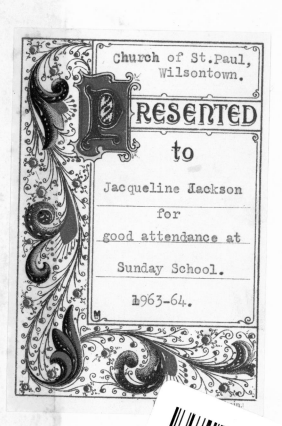

Church of St.Paul,
Wilsontown.

PRESENTED

to

Jacqueline Jackson

for

good attendance at

Sunday School.

1963-64.

SARA GAY – MODEL GIRL
IN NEW YORK

Sara Gay–Model Girl in New York

in New York

by
JANEY SCOTT

Published by
WORLD DISTRIBUTORS (MANCHESTER) LTD.
LONDON—MANCHESTER
ENGLAND

PRINTED IN GREAT BRITAIN
BY CHARLES BIRCHALL & SONS, LTD.,
LIVERPOOL AND LONDON

CONTENTS

CHAPTER I

"SARA! Sara, you're wanted!"

Sara Gay paused in the act of taking off her coat and turned to stare in surprise at the girl who had just burst into the dressing-room. "What on earth's the matter?"

"Mr. Donnell wants you. He's been asking for you for the last twenty minutes and he's livid."

Sara raised her eyebrows and looked at her watch. "I'm not due in until ten and it's only five past. What's all the fuss about?" As she spoke she unzipped her dress and stepped out of it, shivering slightly as the cool air touched her skin. Clad only in brassiére and panties she walked over to a brilliantly lighted mirror and began to smooth her red-gold hair. "Pass me my dressing gown, would you please?"

The other girl complied and Sara put it on, then sat down and carefully began to apply her make-up: a light dusting of powder and lipstick, a heavier application of mascara and green eyeshadow to enhance the colour of her grey-green almond shaped eyes.

All the while the other girl watched in admiration, her mouth a round 'O' of surprise. "I'd never have the pluck to keep Mr. Donnell waiting the way you do. He'll be madder than ever."

"He'd be even more mad if I went up looking unkempt," Sara said placidly. "I did that once when I was a few minutes late and he absolutely tore into me."

She stood up and searched round for the high-heeled black satin pumps which was part of the model-girl uniform when they were on duty. They were lying one against the other in the corner where she had thrown them last night, and she put them on, straightened the seam of her stockings and walked out.

She was half-way along the corridor when a dark-haired girl came running down it.

"Hi," the girl called in an American accent. "I'm terribly late this morning."

"So I see," Sara grinned, "but not to worry. The boss has just asked for me, so you're safe for the next half-hour at least."

This was the other model who shared the dressing-room with Sara in the couturier establishment of Donnell. Betsy had learned modelling in America, but because her father, a U.S. Colonel, was stationed in Europe, she had decided to work in England so that she could see him more frequently. Sara had learned a great deal from Betsy, whose casual disregard for conventions had done a great deal to lighten the hard work and tedium that Sara had experienced in this, her first job.

She sped along the corridor, past the main salon where a customer was already being fitted and upstairs to the studio where Marc Donnell created the fabulous clothes which had made his name a by-word in the world of haute couture.

She tapped on the door and entered. Marc Donnell was seated at a large desk, a drawing-board in front of him, a frown of concentration on his thin, puckish face.

"Where the devil have you been?" he asked irritably.

"I was—"

"Never mind the excuses now. Come and model this toile for me."

He held out a shapeless bundle of white muslin, Sara's first glimpse of one of his new designs.

As she stepped into it, careful not to pull out any of the fragile tacking, she mused on the number of times she would have to wear this particular toile before all the alterations had been finally done to it and it was ready to be made up in its proper material.

"Come on," he said peevishly. "I can't wait all day."

Sara blushed and hurriedly pulled the toile around her shoulders. As she did so a well-built woman in the regulation black dress and pearls worn by all vendeuses, or saleswomen in couturier establishments, stepped forward and helped her.

"Oh good-morning, Mrs. Fielding, I didn't know you were here."

"I've just this minute come in."

Maggie Fielding was Marc Donnell's right hand and to her was left the day-to-day running of the salon. She had been with the young Franco-Irish designer since he had started two years ago and her faith in him had been unshaken from their first moment of meeting. Now, after the brilliant success of his Teen and Twenty Collection in Monte Carlo, she could complacently admit that Marc had "arrived". Indeed it was since the showing of that fabulous Collection that there existed a firm friendship between Mrs. Fielding and Sara. Yet not only was there friendship between her and Mrs. Fielding, but also between herself and Marc. She had lost count of the number of times he had told her that her looks and personality were a constant source of inspiration to him. How wonderful to be able to look on one's job not merely as a source of livelihood but as a pleasure.

But none of these thoughts, strange, exciting thoughts, were apparent in her face as she began to walk up and down in front of Marc Donnell. There was a slight smile on her lips and a twinkle in her eye as she glided across the carpet with her graceful mannequin's walk, paused and turned and walked again. The man at the desk stared at her in fierce concentration, but she knew he was not seeing her at all, only the toile she was wearing.

"There's something the matter with it," he said.

By now Mrs. Fielding had been joined by Hortense, the head fitter, to whom Marc generally gave his most complicated designs. She was a tall, angular Frenchwoman with an excitable temperament, but an infinite capacity for taking pains over detail. In fact it was her love of detail which made her so suitable for her present job, for of all the couturiers Marc Donnell was one who insisted most on exquisite finish for every garment that left his House.

"Personally Monsieur," Hortense said, "I feel the sleeves should be shorter."

Marc put his head on one side and watched Sara as she continued to walk in front of him. "If I make the sleeves shorter I'll have to shorten the hem too, otherwise the whole thing will be out of plumb. No, I don't think it's the sleeves, I think it's—" He snapped his fingers and pushing back his chair advanced on Sara with the scissors in his hand. Without a word he ruthlessly cut the muslin collar around her throat, pulling it back to make the neckline bare. Behind him Hortense and Mrs. Fielding gave little exclamations of admiration as they saw what he had done and as Sara started to walk once more the man himself nodded approval.

It was forty minutes and several alterations later before the three people in the studio declared themselves satisfied with the toile and Sara gently inched her way out of it and slipped on her dressing gown.

Hortense left the studio carrying the toile over her arm and Mrs. Fielding walked over to the far end of the studio and began to look through a selection of material which had been placed on a table in front of the window. Sara had her hand on the door when Marc Donnell called her and she turned to see his rather severe expression relaxed in a smile.

"Don't go for a moment. Come over here and I'll show you my sketches for the rest of the Spring Collection."

Quick to appreciate the honour, she hurried across and bent over the portfolio of drawings. His slim forefinger made quick stabs at each one as he explained the material, elaborating on an accessory. As always when he was concentrating on his work, his brows were drawn together in a fierce frown, his dark eyes glittering with excitement and his short, thick black hair standing on end from his habit of running his fingers through it.

"The theme of the Collection is 'The Young Idea'," he explained, "but instead of concentrating on youth alone, I've added a dash of sophistication."

Sara put down the last drawing and turned to him, her grey-green eyes shining. "They're wonderful! I'm certain they'll be a success."

He grinned. "There's a lot of hard work to get through before they're ready. I hope you're feeling fit."

Sara laughed. "Never felt fitter."

"Good." He patted her shoulder. "It seems only yesterday that we were working on the last Collection. Do you remember it, Sara?"

"I don't think I'll ever forget! But so much has happened since then, hasn't it? You're firmly established now. You've got a backer so you needn't worry about money and all you have to concentrate on is producing the goods."

"That's all," he said drily, and his puckish face had a sudden look of strain which made her realise with instant compunction that though he worked with what appeared to be casualness, it was only a cloak to hide his deep-seated fear of failure.

She left the studio and returned to the dressing-room, but she hardly had a chance to say more than a few words to Betsy before a clock chimed eleven and

Mrs. Fielding put her head round the door to remind them to start showing the Collection. This was a routine part of each day, for the clothes were shown both at eleven a.m. and at three p.m. thus enabling both new and old clients to see every item at their leisure.

Sara had been surprised to discover that though the salon was always packed for the first showing of the Collection, most of the audience comprised buyers and journalists with a smattering of Society women who considered it the done thing to be able to say that they had been at the premiere of Donnell. But the hard core of regular customers preferred to come in later and discuss each dress at length with the particular vendeuse who was attending them.

She had been surprised to realise how many customers relied solely on their vendeuse, and she wished that the same could be said for every one of their clients, for those women who sought no advice were generally the ones who chose the most unsuitable clothes: full-skirted organzas to hide forty-four inch hips; cowl necklines to emphasise bosoms that would have been far better hidden and short skirts to disclose unsightly legs!

This particular morning three clients were in the salon and Sara and Betsy did not finish modelling until half-past twelve, since one of the women insisted on seeing half the things again. However Betsy and Sara's irritation disappeared when Georgina Howard, the other vendeuse in the salon, came to tell them she had managed to sell three suits as well as two evening dresses. Both the girls were delighted for they knew that Mrs. Howard received a commission on her sales and that money would be well-spent in Georgina's case since she was a widow with a five year old girl to bring up.

"It's a pity she doesn't get married again," Sara murmured to Betsy as they walked out through the back of the building and made their way down to an Expresso for lunch.

"She was very much in love with her husband," Betsy responded. "One of the seamstresses told me. She was also very rich too."

"What happened?"

"I'm not sure. It was something to do with the husband's family and some long-standing quarrel."

"Well, maybe she'll meet a millionaire one day," Sara said dreamily. "Then she can come back to Donnell's for all her clothes and give Mrs. Fielding a commission instead!"

"You and your millionaire," Betsy grinned. "You're always trying to match-make. What about yourself?"

"I'm too young for romance," Sara said firmly. "Anyway, I've got my life mapped out. I want to get to the top as a model and then—"

"And then?" Betsy asked as they took their place at a table near the window.

A strange look appeared in Sara's eyes. "I don't know what I'll do then," she confessed. "For the moment, becoming a famous model is the most I can think of."

"And where does Marc Donnell figure in all this? I think your future's tied up with his."

"Don't be silly. Just because I admire him as a designer doesn't mean I admire him as a man."

"But you do though, don't you?"

Sara coloured. "Yes I do, but that still doesn't mean anything. Admiration isn't love. Anyway, you should be the last one to talk. Anyone can see you're sweet on him yourself."

"Much good it does me," said Betsy and stared down at the menu.

Sara looked at her speculatively, for some months ago the girl had admitted that she wished her relationship with Marc Donnell could be more than employer and employee.

"Do you think it's wise to go on working for Marc?" Sara said hesitantly. "I mean it must be awful if you love someone and—and—"

"Don't talk like an idiot," Betsy retorted. "Girls don't pine away from unrequited love these days. At least, *I* don't! Sure I like Marc, but I don't wear my heart on my sleeve and I don't sit at home moping over him. I go out on dates and one day I expect I'll fall in love with somebody else. Till I do I'll just go on carrying the torch for *him*."

"Perhaps if he could be made to see you as a real person and not just as a model," Sara said. "Maybe if I mentioned—"

"Don't you dare mention anything to him," Betsy said vehemently. "If you do, I'll strangle you Sara Gay, I swear it."

"All right, keep your hair on," Sara said. "I was just trying to help."

"Well, don't. I can manage my own affairs. Come

on now, let's give our order or we'll be late getting back and then we'll both be looking for new jobs!"

CHAPTER II

FOR the rest of the afternoon Sara was too busy to ponder over Betsy's problem, but she tucked it into the back of her mind, determined to think about it when she had the time. At four o'clock she was sipping a cup of tea and eating a bun when she was asked to go to Marc's studio.

"Another toile I suppose," she sighed. "I love all the excitement of a new Collection, but all this standing and fitting is terribly tiring."

Betsy nodded. "At times like this I don't envy you being Marc's favourite model!"

Sara was still smiling at this remark as she entered the studio and found the young designer examining a length of black velvet.

"Which colour do you prefer?" he asked as she came forward.

Mystified she stared at what appeared to be two identical lengths of material. "They're both the same, aren't they?"

"Of course not. Look at them carefully."

Sara did so, but could still see no difference.

"There's a world of difference," Marc exclaimed.

"Look at the one on the left. See how much thicker the pile is and look at the black itself, it's deeper with a blue tinge to it, while the one on my right has a grey look."

"I'd never have known if you hadn't told me," she said. "Will it make that much difference to a dress?"

"Of course! This thinner material would crease— apart from which velvet only looks good in deep black. It does something to a woman's skin. Rather like pearls."

"They're my favourite jewels," Sara admitted. "When I was a child I used to long to wear a slinky black velvet dress with a rope of pearls!"

"And have a long jade green cigarette holder too, I don't doubt," Marc said drily, and gave her a shove in the direction of a heap of white muslin lying on his desk. "Slip into that, my girl, and let's have a look at you."

Once more the pattern was repeated. Sara put on the toile and Marc began to alter it, calling both Mrs. Fielding and Hortense into the studio to give their opinions. The only difference with this session and the one that had taken place earlier in the day was that now there were far more toiles to be fitted, and not only was Sara asked to remain in the studio, but Betsy was also called up to model suits and dramatic evening dresses in which she specialised.

As always when he was working Marc was oblivious of time. Down stairs the salon had long since closed, but in the studio the harsh light burned bright and Mrs. Fielding's warm contralto voice could be heard arguing with Hortense's shrill French one over the final details of a particular bodice. Sara and Betsy were too tired to think and did what they were supposed to do like automatons. Not for the world would either of them have mentioned that they were dizzy with hunger or sick with fatigue, so intent were they on helping this young man in whom they both believed.

It was left to Mrs Fielding, her motherly instincts aroused at the sight of the girls' pale faces, to remind Marc that it was well past eight o'clock.

"Good Lord, I'd no idea of the time." He put his scissors down on the desk. "Why didn't you tell me before?"

"I forgot," the vendeuse admitted, "but I'm not as young as you three and I can't stand up to these long hours any more. I think we should call it a day. There's no need to work at such a pace, Marc, the Collection is months away yet."

"I know, but once I've got my ideas on paper I can't wait to see them executed." He ran his hands through his hair. "Still, I suppose you're right, we might as well pack it up."

"I don't mind staying if you want to do any more work," Betsy volunteered.

"That's sweet of you," Marc said casually, "but if I wanted anyone to stay behind it would be Sara. I've a couple of ideas I'd like to work out on her."

Although she felt sorry for Betsy, Sara could not help a thrill of elation that Marc should single her out. But to hide her embarrassment she made a joke of it. "When you say you want to work things out on me, you make me feel like a prize fighter!"

"You know what I mean," he grinned. "I like draping material around you and seeing the way it falls. It gives me inspiration. Come up to my flat and I'll fix some supper for you, then we can get back to work."

Sara looked at Betsy, and the American girl shrugged.

"Well, if you don't need me anymore I guess I'll push off."

Mrs. Fielding and Hortense left the studio together a couple of minutes later, leaving Marc and Sara alone.

"This is like old times, isn't it?" he said to her and led her up to his flat on the topmost floor of the house.

Sara followed him into the large living-cum-dining-room where he spent his leisure hours. She had been here many times before, though always on occasions like this when they had been working late, and she turned on the table lamps and put a Beethoven Sonata on the record player.

Soon an appetising smell came from the small modern kitchen on the far side of the living-room. At one time Sara would have offered to help Marc, but she knew better now, realising that he found it relaxing to potter about among food: beating eggs, mixing flour, adding pungent herbs and finally bringing to the table the most aromatic of dishes. Tonight was no exception and as they sat down to a meal of casseroled lamb with garlic bread and French salad, she found herself almost bursting with delight.

"Coming to work for you was the best stroke of luck that ever happened to me," she said out loud.

"I'm not sure the luck was on your side. You're a wonderful model, Sara. You could find a much better paid job and a much easier one too."

"I'm not looking for an easy job. I'm looking for a job I enjoy doing. And you don't need me to tell you how much I enjoy working for you, do you?"

"No, I don't. You make your delight obvious." He leaned across the table and touched her cheek. "You're a sweet kid, Sara. I'll have to watch out not to take advantage of you and overwork you."

She smiled and said nothing, knowing that the moment the meal was over he would be aching to return to the studio. She was proved right in this, for hardly had she finished her coffee when she saw his brows draw together impatiently and out of the corner of her eye noticed his fingers drumming on the side of his chair.

"You and your hints," she giggled. "Come on, you won't be at rest until you're back in the studio."

Hand in hand they ran down the stairs and set to work again. In silence he draped different brocades over Sara's figure, pinning a fold of it here, tying a fold of it there and stepping back each time to survey what he had done. Painstakingly one more design was created and it was not until he carefully helped her out of the material that she was able to look at her watch and see the time. Eleven-thirty!

"The hostel!" she cried in dismay. "We've done it again!"

Sara lived in a hostel some fifteen minutes from the salon and though admirable in every respect, it had one major difficulty as far as her job was con-

cerned: the doors closed at eleven on week nights and
eleven-thirty during the week-end. Generally this did
not bother her since she liked to be in bed early, but
at times like this—when Marc was working on his
Collection—she was apt to stay in the studio until
midnight and this led to many complications.

On one occasion when she had been so late she had
spent the night at Mrs. Fielding's flat and when it had
occurred again, rather than bother the vendeuse, she
had pounded on the door of the hostel until one of the
girls had heard her and come down to let her in. The
warden had heard her too and Sara had not forgotten
the interview she had had with the woman, who had
made it clear that job or no job she could not make
exceptions for anyone.

"We have to close the doors at eleven," she had explained firmly. "These are the rules laid down by the
Board of Governors. If you have the sort of job that
necessitates your coming in later than eleven then
you'll have to find somewhere else to live. There's a
long list of girls waiting to fill your vacancy and . . . ."

Realising the futility of arguing, Sara had vowed
not to be late any more. And now she had done
it again!

"There's no help for it," Marc said flatly. "We'll
have to ring Mrs. Fielding and ask her to put you
up."

"I hate disturbing her," Sara said wretchedly.

"It can't be helped. It seems to me you'd better find
somewhere else to stay in London. That hostel of
yours is ridiculous."

"It's comfortable and cheap. And besides, my parents wouldn't let me live alone. They were quite explicit on the terms that they would let me work in London, and that was one of them."

"You and your parents," Marc sighed. "Come on, infant. I'll ring Maggie and tell her I'm bringing you over."

Sara spent the night in Mrs Fielding's flat in Kensington and the two of them travelled to work together the next morning.

"It's funny you should have spent the night with me," the woman said as they jogged in the bus down Knightsbridge. "I was thinking about it the other day and wondering how you'd manage about your curfew once Marc started working on his new Collection. In fact I nearly told you about a flat someone wants to let."

"I could never take a flat on my own," Sara said regretfully. "Apart from Mummy and Daddy not letting me, I couldn't afford it."

"But that's just the point, this flat's big enough to share with another girl. Surely your parents wouldn't object to that?"

"Not if they approved of the girl," Sara admitted, her pulses quickening with interest. "Where is it?"

"In the same block as mine. That's how I heard of it. The rent's six guineas a week, so if you shared it with someone else it would only cost you three."

"That's exactly what I'm paying now," Sara said. "It sounds simply marvellous."

"It *is* marvellous," came the answer. "It's beautifully furnished and the people who own it are not interested in making any profit as long as they let it to

the right sort of people. They're going abroad for
three years and want to sub-let it."

"Oh, don't go on," Sara pleaded. "You're making
me feel awful. I just don't know anyone who could
share it with me."

"What about Betsy?"

"She's already sharing a flat with another American
girl."

"Haven't you any other friends?"

"Not in London. All my friends are in Frimpton."

"Of course, I was forgetting you're a country girl."

"Not a country girl," Sara laughed. "Frimpton's a
seaside town."

The bus swung into Park Lane and within a few
moments they had left it behind and were walking
down Curzon Street towards Shepherd's Market. On
and off during the rest of the day Sara thought of the
flat and her determination to take it grew so fierce that
she could think of nothing else. Just before lunch she
waylaid the vendeuse and asked her if she could go
and see it.

"Of course, my dear. I'll find out." Mrs Fielding
went into the small room which she and Georgina
Howard shared. Each vendeuse had a desk of her own
in which she kept the names of her clients, a list of the
clothes that each one had ordered and all the special
trimmings that went with every garment. To the vendeuse was given the task of matching up all the fabrics and seeing that the clients' requests were carried
out properly in the work-room, and many were the
times Sara had seen the normally placid Mrs. Fielding
lose her temper with a button-maker who had sent the

wrong buttons for the dress of one of her clients, or the gentle Georgina Howard burst into a torrent of furious Italian with a young embroiderer who had put silver bugles on the bodice of a dress instead of pink ones.

But now the vendeuses' room was empty and Mrs. Fielding dialled a number and spoke on the telephone.

"You're in luck Sara," she said as she replaced the receiver. "Mrs. Willow is home so if you'd like to go along right away . . . ."

"Thanks awfully, I'll go at once."

It was one o'clock when Sara arrived at the block of mansion flats where Mrs. Fielding lived. The one she wanted was on the top floor, set at the end of a long corridor. It was the smallest flat in the building so Mrs. Willow said, but it was also one of the sunniest. There was a large bedroom and an equally large sitting-room furnished in gay-patterned chintz and a mushroom-pink carpet. The kitchen was a delight and so was the large ginger cat purring happily in front of the fire. Through the wide windows the Autumn sunlight shone mellow, illuminating the patina of the beautiful antique furniture and gleaming on the Georgian silver teapot on the sideboard.

"It's a beautiful flat," Sara breathed, "and so cheap too."

"We're not letting the flat to make money," Mrs. Willow explained. "As I said to Mrs. Fielding, we really want someone who'll take care of the place for us and treat it as if it's their home."

"Oh I'd do that," Sara said. "I really would."

"I'm sure you would." The woman touched her

shoulder. "I'd love you to live here, my dear. I'd feel quite happy to go away and know that you were taking care of things for us and particularly of Tommy."

"Tommy?" Sara said questioningly, and knew the answer almost at once, for the cat, hearing its name, arched its tail and began to purr. "Oh Tommy!" she repeated with a laugh, and picking him up hugged him close. "I'd certainly take care of Tommy."

"Well, now I know you like cats the whole thing's settled," Mrs. Willow said. "The flat is yours. You can have vacancy a week from today. I'll speak to the Agents and if you could tell me who your solicitors are we'll get in touch with them right away and fix things up."

Sara gave the name of the firm of solicitors where she had worked in Frimpton, and in a daze, said goodbye to Mrs. Willow and returned to the salon.

Mrs. Fielding was waiting for her as she came into the dressing-room. "Well, did you like it?"

"It was wonderful and I've agreed to take it."

"Have you now?" Mrs. Fielding said in astonishment. "*You're* a fast worker. Only this morning you said you didn't have anyone who could share it with you."

It was a second or two before the words penetrated Sara's mind and as they did so, the euphoria which had surrounded her since leaving the flat began to dissolve and she came face to face with reality. It was singularly unpleasant.

"Gosh!" she said. "I'd completely forgotten!"

"Well, you're in a fine pickle. You've given your

word to take the flat and you can't back out of it now.
What are you going to do?"

"I don't know." Sara's chin tilted defiantly. "But one
thing's certain. I'm not giving up that flat. I'll find
someone to share it with me if it's the last thing I do!"

CHAPTER III

ON Friday afternoon Sara returned to Frimpton for the week-end. The problem of the flat had loomed large in her mind for the whole of the week, and though she had asked all the girls at the hostel whom she liked—and some she did not like overmuch— she'd still not been able to find anyone to share it with her.

"If the worst comes to the worst," she thought, "I'll have to live there on my own."

But even as she thought it she knew it was impossible for not only would it take half her salary, but would also mean a row with her parents. Yet the more she thought about it, the more determined she became to find a way out and she was still mulling over the problem when she reached the small, semi-detached house that stood in the curving crescent overlooking the rain-washed Channel. Once inside the hall, with her mother hugging her and her father pinching her cheek, to say nothing of her brother rummaging through her pockets to see what she had brought him, Sara momentarily forgot her problems, though it came back with full force when, supper over and her young brother safely in bed, she sat in front of the fire with her parents.

"What's worrying you dear?" Mrs Gay asked gently. "When you get that funny little frown between your eyes I know something's on your mind."

"It's so difficult to keep a secret from you," Sara sighed. "But you're quite right. I *am* worried." Hesitantly at first, and then more quickly once she had begun, she told her mother and father about the flat.

"It's absolutely beautiful," she said, "and it'll be the end if I can't take it."

"You're not living alone and that's final," her mother said in a no-nonsense voice. "We agreed to all that when we let you go to London."

Tears came into Sara's eyes and she rubbed them away angrily. "But I'll never find anything like it again. It's a bargain, a downright bargain. It's beautifully furnished, it's got central heating and constant hot water and a lift and a porter and—"

"All right, my girl, you needn't go on," her father said. "I'm quite sure it has all mod cons. The only thing it hasn't got is someone for you to share it with!"

Realising the truth of his words Sara nodded miserably and stared into the depths of the fire. The orange flames doubled and then trembled as tears would not refuse to be held back. How awful to find such a gem then have to turn it down. Misery grew upon misery and she sank lower in her chair.

Mr. Gay looked across at his wife and then at his daughter. He opened his mouth to speak but his words were forestalled by the ringing of the telephone, and with a mutter of relief he went to answer it.

"It's for you Sara," he called. "Beryl Radford."

Sara jumped up. Beryl was her best friend and at one time they had worked together in a solicitor's office. Indeed it was due to Beryl that Sara was now a model, for it had been her friend who had urged her to enter for a beauty contest which resulted in her winning first prize, thus receiving a sum of money sufficient to enrol her at the Lena Lane Model School.

She picked up the receiver, her voice listless as she said hello.

"What's the matter with *you*?" Beryl's voice was bubbling and full of vitality.

"Everything." Succinctly Sara told her friend what had happened.

"What hard lines," Beryl said. "But it won't do any good moping about it. Come on over and let's have a yarn."

"Not tonight. I feel too rotten. But I'll see you in the morning. Are you working?"

"Not this Saturday, thank goodness. I'll meet you for coffee in the usual place."

Feeling a little more cheered, Sara put down the telephone. Strange how Beryl had the aptitude to make one feel better. Maybe it was because she was always so good-humoured and placid.

Promptly at eleven next morning Sara pushed open the glass door of Frimpton's smartest café. Not that it was smart compared with even the most ordinary London Expresso bar, for the décor was decidedly old-fashioned and the coffee more like dishwater than the strong Italian to which she had now become accustomed.

But everything was forgotten at the sight of Beryl's plump, smiling face, and Sara hurried over to the table in the corner and hugged her happily.

"Gosh, it's good to see you," she said. "I miss your ugly face!"

"I miss yours," Beryl said happily, and went on munching a cake. "I've ordered coffee for us and scones. I know they're your favourites."

Sara nodded and the two girls began to talk animatedly. It was amazing the things they had to say to one another, things that could not be written, no matter how long their letters. It was nearly twelve o'clock before they fell silent and Sara leaned back in her chair and sighed.

"You know, Beryl, I miss you."

"I miss *you* even more. At least you've got a job that keeps you happy, but mine is as dull as ditchwater. I've often thought of packing it in and coming to London."

There was a moment of silence and both girls stared at one another. In Sara's face was a look of wonder, in Beryl's a look of fear as she saw what Sara was thinking.

"Now don't take me seriously," she said quickly. "I didn't mean it. My folks would never let me—"

"Of course they'd let you. You don't want to spend your life mouldering away in a dusty old solicitor's office, do you? Why, you could get a job in London for twice as much as you earn here."

"And spend twice as much to keep myself."

"Not if you share a flat with me." Sara clutched her friend's hand. "Don't you want to live in London?"

"I'd love nothing more. It's just that I've never been away from home . . . ."

"Well, you're a big girl now and it's time you behaved like one." Sara signalled the waitress for the bill and pushed back her chair. "Come on, I'm going to talk to your mother. Once she's said you can come your father's bound to agree."

For once Sara was right in her assumption that everything would work out well, for Mrs. Radford seemed delighted for her daughter to work in London, and by the time Sara left Frimpton on Sunday evening everything had been settled. Beryl would give a week's notice to her firm and she and Sara would take over the Willow flat the following Monday.

"I'll ring up some employment agencies as soon as I get back," Sara promised her friend, "and I'll tell them the sort of job you're looking for. I'm sure you won't find it difficult to get a place."

"I don't mind what I take," Beryl said excitedly. "Anything'll be acceptable as long as it doesn't involve working in a solicitor's office."

Promptly at nine-thirty on Monday morning Sara, armed with a load of pennies, stepped into the telephone box opposite the salon and began to dial some employment agencies. To all of them she gave Beryl's qualifications and was greatly reassured when everyone to whom she spoke told her there would be no difficulty in placing a girl with such a high shorthand and typing speed and a reference of three years. Sara then dialled Mrs. Willow and confirmed that she and her friend would be arriving at the flat the following week.

"You can come on the Sunday night," Mrs. Willow told her. "My husband and I can quite easily leave then and I'm sure it will be more convenient for you."

"It certainly would," Sara agreed. "It means I won't have to ask Mrs. Fielding for any time off."

Happily she left the kiosk and sped across the road to Donnell's. It was unbelievable the way things were falling into place. She must be the luckiest girl alive.

Mrs Fielding was delighted when she learned that Sara had found someone to share the flat with her, and Betsy gave a whoop of excitement.

"Gee, you'll sure be able to live it up once you're out of that hostel!"

"I don't want to live anything up," Sara protested. "I just want a nice quiet life."

"You don't do too badly, what with Marc and Peter."

"Peter!" At the mention of his name Sara gave an exclamation. How remiss of her not to have telephoned him to say she was going home for the weekend. Still, he usually called her at Frimpton if he could not reach her at the hostel, and she wondered why he had not done so. Probably short of cash, if she knew anything of her young friend!

Although he was beginning to achieve success as a photographer, he was still finding commissions coming in more slowly than he had anticipated, one of the reasons being that his studio was in Balham, which many of the fashion houses considered too far out to send their models.

Guiltily she blamed herself for his straitened circumstances. She had first met him when she had finished her training at the Lena Lane Model School and had been desperately searching for a job, unable to understand why, as the most successful pupil in her course, she alone of all the class was still without a job. She had bumped—quite literally—into Peter Redgrave one morning when she had gone to the Agency to see if they had any news for her, and when the young man with the tousled brown hair had picked her up from the floor where he had knocked her, she had shown him her photographs, photographs which had been circulated to all the fashion houses requiring a model.

He had taken one look at them and pulled a face. "They're phoney and artificial," he had said. "Let *me* take some of you and I guarantee you'll get a job at once!"

Discovering he worked for Lucien, the very photographer who had taken the stilted snaps which he was now criticising, she had eagerly agreed to let Peter take some new pictures. The results more than justified her hopes, for they had helped her to get a job at Donnell's. Unfortunately Lucien discovered what Peter had done, and in a fit of rage, fired him. Left to his own resources, Peter set himself up in a dingy basement in Balham. At first the going had been difficult but now he was becoming better known, and though Sara wished he would shoot to fame like a meteorite, Peter himself was well satisfied with his progress.

"Hey, come back to this world!" Betsy's voice

broke into Sara's thoughts and with a start she realised that the other girl was speaking to her.

"I'm sorry," she apologised. "I was thinking about Peter."

"That's pretty obvious from the starry look in your eyes."

Sara blushed and shook her head, knowing better than to try and explain to Betsy that all she felt for Peter was sisterly affection. Betsy would never believe such a thing possible, for though she had said her heart was given to Marc she still managed to have a gay time with a host of other admirers.

Slipping on her green silk wrapper, Sara began the daily task of making-up, wondering what the rest of the day held in store for her. She did not have to wonder for long, for almost immediately she received a summons to go to the studio.

The rest of the week followed a similar course and by Friday she was so tired that all she longed for was a week-end in bed. It was not an easy thing to do at the hostel for though she had a cubicle to herself, the walls were so thin that every sound could be heard, making rest, let alone sleep, well-nigh impossible until everyone had settled down at eleven o'clock.

"This time next week-end," she promised herself, "I'll be able to lie in my own room in my own flat and do exactly as I want. What fun it's going to be to share a place with Beryl. Why, it's the first time we've really been alone together. No parents telling us what to do, no kid brothers interfering and prying. What bliss— what utter bliss!"

CHAPTER IV

ON Sunday afternoon Beryl's parents drove her up in their car, complete with luggage, a basket of cooked food and a portable television.

"A present from my father," she whispered to Sara as they hugged one another outside the hostel. "He obviously thinks it'll encourage me to stay in nights!"

Giggling, Sara loaded her luggage into the boot and then directed Mr. Radford to the block of flats.

By six o'clock they were unpacked and sitting down to an early supper in the alcove dining-room.

Beryl's parents were charmed by everything and her mother looked longingly at the eye-level gas cooker and the beautifully equipped kitchen.

"How lucky you are. Here am I, married for twenty-three years, and still using the same old oven!"

"I'll let you come up and cook us a dinner occasionally," Beryl giggled.

"When I come up and see you I'll expect *you* to cook the dinner," her mother retorted, and unexpectedly her eyes glistened with tears. "I do hope you'll be all right together," she said anxiously. "You're so young to be alone."

"We're not alone," Beryl said stoutly. "And dash it all, we can't be tied to our parents' apron strings for ever."

"That's quite right," her father said, and put his arm around his wife's shoulder. "You're not crying for Beryl, my dear, you're crying because your little bird is spreading her wings and leaving the nest."

"Don't be ridiculous," Mrs. Radford sniffed. But her husband's words had a salutary effect, for she wiped her eyes and made no more reference to her daughter's departure.

It was nine o'clock before they left to return to Frimpton, enjoining Beryl to come home any week-end.

"Every week-end, in fact," her mother said. "And if you haven't got the train fare, just let me know and I'll—"

"If I haven't got the train fare," Beryl said firmly, "I won't come down. I'm on my own now and I can manage all right. Sara's got a whole list of jobs for me to go and see tomorrow and I'm sure I'll be able to find one right away."

Finally with the door closed and the sound of footsteps echoing down the corridor, the two girls looked at one another, for the first time realising they were on their own. A momentary feeling of panic overwhelmed Sara, and then her sense of humour came to her aid, and catching Beryl around her plump shoulders she danced her across the hall and into the living-room, swinging her round and round until they both collapsed on the settee.

It did not take long for them to develop a routine.

Beryl started work as secretary in a theatrical agency, a job which afforded her close-ups of some of the most popular singers of the day. Within a few weeks she was secretary to the head of the agency himself, and this meant a rise in pay which brought her earnings on a level with Sara's.

They had divided the chores of the flat between them, though Beryl firmly said she intended to do the bulk of the cooking when Sara was working on a Collection.

"Quite often I don't have anything to do all day," she explained. "But when your Mr. Donnell's working on a Collection I know you're pretty hard pressed, and it seems silly for you to have to come back and start doing things around here."

"It doesn't seem fair to leave it to you though," Sara protested.

"Fair or not, that's the way I want it. Anyway, I love cooking, and I only wish I could do more of it."

"I'm jolly glad you can't," Sara said frankly. "You eat too much as it is."

Guiltily Beryl's hand, which had been hovering over a chocolate box in her lap, dropped to her side and she looked down at her plump figure.

"I keep meaning to diet, but I never get around to it."

Sara held her tongue, unwilling to hurt her friend by being too frank. Perhaps when Beryl had lived in London longer and became more fashion-conscious she would want to diet of her own accord.

Now that she had somewhere to entertain, Sara invited Betsy over for lunch most Sundays, and also invited Georgina Howard and Maggie Fielding to supper. Marc Donnell came over too and Beryl served up a meal so superlative that he had commented on it. Peter was the only one of her friends who had not yet been to the flat, for the week she had moved in he had received a commission to fly to Rome to take some photographs, and he expected to be away a month.

It was amazing how quickly the weeks passed, and almost before she was aware of it shop windows were displaying figures of Santa Claus while the plate glass was covered with cotton wool snow. Three more shopping weeks to Christmas ran the placards, and Sara began to write lists of presents, scratching off each name as it was completed, but always finding a fresh name to add to it.

In the salon preparations for the Collection had now reached the third and final stage, and two additional models had been temporarily hired. Some of the clothes were altered to fit them, thus obviating the necessity for Sara and Betsy to put in more than eighteen hours a day! Not that either of them minded, caught up as they were in the excitement and expectancy of the new line. They both realised how important its success was to Marc, for though James Beresford, his financial backer, was his most devoted admirer, Odette Beresford the wife, still had reservations about him, due in the main to her desire for her husband to back Paul Gerard, the French designer for whom she had worked as a vendeuse until her marriage less than a year ago.

"Do you remember how livid Mrs. Beresford was when Marc got more applause than Paul Gerard at that dress show in Monte Carlo?" Sara remarked one afternoon in the middle of December as she was putting on her coat preparatory to going home.

"I sure do." Betsy flicked a comb through her dark curls. "I don't think I'll ever forget the horror I felt when we discovered Marc's most beautiful clothes had been slashed by that Nina Durack. What a beastly girl she was. I wonder what she's doing now that Paul Gerard's sacked her."

"She probably got a modelling job somewhere else. She's very good, you know," Sara said more generously than she felt. "If we hadn't been at the Model School together I'm sure she'd have won the Gold Medal instead of me."

"Well she didn't," Betsy said firmly. "That's probably why she's such an enemy of yours."

Sara pushed aside all thoughts of the tall, languid girl who had been such a thorn in her flesh from their first moment of meeting—bad enough to think of Nina when she met her, without thinking of her when she was no longer on her immediate horizon.

"What about coming to the flat for coffee tonight?" she asked as they walked down the main staircase.

"Thanks honey, but I've got a date. A real devastating guy. He's over here on a three month course from Harvard University."

"You and your devastating guys?" Sara laughed and waved goodbye as she boarded a bus going down Park Lane.

It was pleasant to jog through the busy streets and look out of the window at the brightly lighted shops. Occasionally when they stopped for the traffic lights she would get a better look at some of the windows and saw with interest that many of the dresses were copies of Marc's last Collection. Not that any copy could do justice to his original models, she conceded, for all Marc's clothes had a superior cut and detailed finish. "What would the public think of his new Collection?" she wondered and was still wondering about it when she left the bus and walked down the tree-lined road to the mansion block.

The moment she inserted her key in the lock and opened the front door, she knew from the appetising smell of cooking that wafted out of the tiny hall, that Beryl was in. The next moment the plump figure of her friend, an apron round her waist and fork in her hand, emerged from the kitchen.

"I thought I heard you," she remarked cheerfully. "The food's nearly ready."

Sara took off her hat and tossed it on the hall table. "Give me a minute, will you? I'm too fagged to eat yet."

Beryl followed her into the living-room and watched as she flopped into an armchair and kicked her shoes off.

"Oh, my poor aching feet!" Sara groaned. "This is almost as bad as being a nurse."

"Not as satisfying though. At least when you're a nurse you're helping others."

"I'm helping people in *this* job," Sara protested. "Fashion's an important morale builder, Beryl. Why, do you know that in lots of hospitals and mental homes they give courses to their patients on beauty treatment and dress-making?"

"No, I didn't," Beryl conceded. "But I suppose you're right. I know I always feel much better myself once I've got some lipstick on and I'm wearing a decent dress."

"There you are then," Sara said triumphantly, "so don't tell me my work isn't rewarding."

"Sorry, old girl." The sound of sizzling came from the kitchen and with a cry Beryl disappeared. "Don't be too long resting," she called through the half open door, "or supper will get spoilt."

"You might as well serve it now," Sara said as an appetising aroma wafted out to her. "I think a good meal is the only thing to stop me feeling tired."

While they were eating the girls discussed their working day and Beryl recounted a meeting she had witnessed between her boss and a prominent variety star. She was an observant girl and a good mimic and several times Sara's laugh rang out.

"And now let's hear about *your* glamorous day," Beryl concluded as she pushed her plate aside.

Sara grimaced. "Most of the glamour's in the eye of the beholder. I've never worked so hard in my life as I did this afternoon."

"But it's fun too," Beryl said. "All those gorgeous clothes you wear . . ." She glanced at her own plump form and sighed. "Not that they'd look anything on me even if I could afford them. With my face and figure it doesn't matter what I wear."

"You're so wrong!" In her vehemence Sara banged the table with her fist, making the coffee cups rattle. "Oh, I admit you couldn't look like a model, but why should you want to? You could look jolly attractive if you only went about things in the right way. I never said anything to you before because I didn't want to risk hurting your feelings, but—well—you wear all the wrong things."

She stopped and looked at her friend fearfully, afraid she might have gone too far, but Beryl's expression remained as placid as ever.

"Don't be an ass Sara, you know I'm not touchy. As a matter of fact, I'd be jolly pleased if you'd give me a few hints. I know I wear the wrong clothes, but I can never tell why."

"Well, I'll tell you. You try to ape other people. Take the dress you're wearing now for instance." She fingered the tight-fitting black dress Beryl was wearing. "It's jolly nice but it doesn't happen to be *you*. It's the sort of thing a slender, sophisticated girl should wear. You should go in for more casual clothes, and not have them so tight-fitting. It's much more slimming to wear loose things than to squeeze yourself into skin-tight sheaths that show all the bulges."

"I suppose you're right," Beryl sighed. "But I guess every girl has a secret urge to be glamorous."

"Maybe they do, but not every boy wants a glamorous girl-friend. In fact most of the boys I know are put off by the fact that I've got a glamorous job—they're afraid I won't spoil my beautiful white hands at the kitchen sink. Why, most men who ask me for dates are either middle-aged wolves or philandering playboys! So you see, it's not all honey being a glamour girl."

"All right, I'll let you come with me next time I buy some new clothes." Beryl began to clear the table. "Now how about bringing your beautiful white hands to the kitchen sink and helping me with the dishes?"

Sara laughed. "I really should do the lot myself. After all you cooked the meal."

"Never mind." Beryl shook the soap powder into a bowl of steaming water and whisked it into a lather with a washing-up mop. "Sometimes I think—" She stopped as the door bell rang. "Are you expecting anyone?"

"Not a soul. I'll go and see who it is."

She disappeared down the corridor, returning a moment later with a young man about her own height. "Beryl, it's Peter Redgrave, I don't think you know him."

Beryl smiled at the newcomer. "No but I've heard so much about you that I feel I do. Sorry I can't shake hands." She spread her soapy palms wide in explanation and turned to her friend. "Why don't you take him into the sitting-room and as soon as I've finished this I'll make some coffee."

"I can't wait that long!" Grinning, Peter tossed the portfolio he was carrying on to the table and seizing a frilly apron from behind the door, tied it around his waist. Then picking up a tea-cloth he strode over to the sink and began to polish a plate vigorously. "What you girls need is a man around the house!"

"Suits me," Sara grinned. "Especially if he's as domesticated as you."

She began to prepare the coffee and Beryl, as she washed up, stole covert glances at the boy beside her. He had the stocky build of a footballer and light brown hair flopped over his forehead. His square jaw was fringed with a stubbly beard and though he was by no means handsome, there was something engaging about his countenance which she liked.

"How did the Rome trip go?" Sara asked a few minutes later as she carried a tray with coffee cups into the sitting-room and began to pour out.

"Very well, thanks." Peter went into the kitchen and came back with the portfolio. "I brought these to show you."

Sara took the folder and began to leaf through the prints, exclaiming in delight as she saw the unconventional, yet beautiful shots of Rome with the model girls all wearing delightful Italian sweaters and knitted clothes.

"So that's what you went over for! Was it a proper commission?"

"You bet your life," Peter grinned. "The Editor of *Dress* herself asked me to do it and paid me on the nail too. In fact I've done so well out of it that I suggest taking you both out to supper tomorrow night if you're free."

"There's no need to take me," Beryl protested. "I don't want to play gooseberry!"

"Who said anything about gooseberry? I'd like to be seen with two pretty girls at the same time. It would do my ego no end of good."

Beryl did not protest further, but her cheeks were red as she sipped her coffee and made a pretence of looking at a magazine. Peter strolled over to the wireless and switched it on. The strains of a Cha-Cha filtered into the room and he pulled Sara to her feet and began to dance. When the song came to an end he seized Beryl round the waist and swept her up against him.

"This is a Samba," she cried. "I can't do it."

"Neither can I, but what does it matter?"

Giggling helplessly, Beryl tried to follow him and though she did not do too badly, she was thankful when the invisible band switched to a quick-step.

It was past midnight when Peter took his leave and nearly half-an-hour later before Sara and Beryl were ready for bed. As Sara stretched out an arm to switch off the light she stopped and looked at her friend.

"Do you know something—on the way home to-night I decided to go to bed early. Ten o'clock was going to be my dead-line—and here it is already half-past twelve. Whatever happened to this evening?"

Beryl did not answer. She was already asleep and from the smile that curved the corners of her mouth it was obvious that she was enjoying a very pleasant dream.

CHAPTER V

SARA and Beryl returned to Frimpton for Christmas and Sara in particular was glad that the holiday was a quiet one. It was only when she relaxed over the five day period that she realised how tired she was and how intense had been the strain of the last few weeks. Thank goodness that when she returned to Donnell's there would be no more fittings. Marc had announced himself finally satisfied with his Collection and all that was left now was to show it to the public and hope it would be a success.

As always when she was away from the salon for more than a couple of days, she felt a longing to be back and after a week-end at home began to count the hours until she could return to London. Yet was it the salon calling her back or was it the young designer who owned it?

Marc was spending Christmas with his mother in Paris and Sara had been disappointed when she had heard for she had toyed with the idea of asking him to spend Christmas with her own family. Indeed the request had been on her lips when he had mentioned that he was going to Paris, on the night flight of that same evening.

But her disappointment had been mitigated by her pleasure at his Christmas present: a beautiful gold brooch with her initials 'S' and 'G' marked out in tiny emeralds.

"To match your eyes," he explained.

"How perfectly wonderful!" she gasped. "I've never had anything so exquisite."

"You will, infant," he promised.

She looked at him startled, and saw a strange expression on his face.

"Why do you say that Marc?"

He shrugged. "You're very innocent, Sara. So innocent that you don't realise what a wonderful model you are. And you haven't reached maturity yet. When you do you'll have everyone at your feet—and by everyone I mean men."

"Oh men! If you think they'll be able to bowl me over with presents, you'd better think again." She flung her arms wide. "Sable, mink, diamonds and pearls—they'll all be sent back."

"You might change your mind once you actually receive them!"

"Never! Taking presents from people puts you under an obligation to them, and that's something I'd hate."

"You don't feel that way about this gift, do you?" he asked anxiously. "You're not under any obligation to me, Sara. I know you could get a much better paid job and if you want to leave at any time—"

"Whatever brought this up?" she asked in astonishment. "I love working for you. I told you Marc, you're going to the top and I'm going there with you. We're

half-way there already." She rummaged in the pocket
of her dress and handed him a small leather box.
"Here's *your* present. Nothing as magnificent as the
one you've given me, but . . . ."

Marc took the box and opened it, staring down at a
pair of mother-of-pearl cuff-links. Without a word he
took them out and removing the ones he was wearing,
replaced them with Sara's. Then he came over and
gently kissed her on the tip of her nose.

"I'll wear them all the time," he said solemnly, "and
they'll remind me of you."

Sara remembered these words as she returned to
Donnell's after the Christmas holiday. The house was
a hive of activity for Marc had decided to have the
entrance hall redecorated. The walls were covered
with silver and grey striped paper and in place of the
crystal chandelier there swung a Regency brass lamp.

"Do you approve?" a voice asked behind her, and
she swung round to see Marc.

"Oh I do," she enthused.

"Good." He preceded her up the stairs, nodding to
a couple of workmen. "They should be finished in
another few days," he explained. "Their boss is a
friend of mine and he got his men to work during part
of the holidays."

"You have friends in all sorts of places," she teased.

"Naturally! It's stupid just to cultivate the best
people, for the best people aren't always the most
helpful!"

Laughing together they walked along the corridor
and as Marc strode on to his studio, Sara entered the
dressing-room.

As the date of the Collection drew nearer the tension increased to fever-pitch and by the time the actual day dawned everyone's nerves were stretched to breaking point.

Sara arrived at Donnell's extra early, but Mrs. Fielding was already there and from the look of her it appeared she had not gone home the night before.

"What a night it's been," she confided. "At the last minute Marc decided he didn't like one of the dresses and unpicked the whole thing."

"Is it one of mine?" Sara asked in consternation.

"No, it's one of Betsy's. Anyway, I must say Marc was right, as usual. The dress looks much better now he's redone it." She gave Sara a little push. "Hurry up, child, and get ready. We're due to start at eleven."

"There's an hour yet," Sara protested.

"Maybe so, but you won't have the dressing-room to yourself, remember."

Sara made a face for she had forgotten she would have to share the small room with the temporary models, to say nothing of the head fitter and her assistant, as well as the two girls who were in charge of all the accessories and whose duty it was to see that before each mannequin stepped out of the salon she was wearing the correct hat, shoes, gloves and jewellery to go with her outfit.

The dressing-room was a scene of pandemonium. Chairs were heaped with models' own clothes while the ones due to be shown hung on rails around the room, jealousy guarded by the two fitters. Sara squeezed herself in and inching over to the mirror began to apply her make-up. She took extra care with

it, applying her mascara thickly and making sure that
the arch of her eyebrows was not too heavy. Thank
goodness I don't have to bother overmuch with my
hair, she thought as she brushed it out vigorously and
let it fall the way it wished.

One of the other girls watched her enviously and
echoed Sara's thoughts.

"How lucky to have naturally wavy hair. I have to
set mine every four days and when I'm modelling for
something special like this, I sleep in pins the night
before!"

Sara looked sympathetic but had no time for conversation for Mrs. Fielding came in to say they were
ready.

Sara peeped out of the dressing-room and heard the
hum of conversation coming from the salon. It was
packed with people sitting on small, gilt chairs which
had been ordered especially for the occasion. The
air was heavy with the scent of flowers and perfume
and she breathed in deep and felt her pulses quicken.
On the next floor a group of seamstresses peered over
the banisters, eager for the first glimpse of the man-
nequins wearing the models over which they had
laboured so long. Another seamstress came running
down the stairs carrying a final dress with her; it was
shrouded in white muslin to make sure no prying eyes
should catch a glimpse of it too soon. Sara stepped
aside to let her come into the dressing-room and then
moved over to put on the first dress she was to show,
a tangerine organza Ascot dress with vivid blue accessories—such an unusual colour combination that she
could remember Mrs. Fielding's scream of horror

when it had first been mooted. Now, as she gave herself a final inspection in the mirror before stepping out, she had to admit that Marc had been right as usual.

Although she was always nervous before she had to appear in front of an audience, the moment she entered the salon and walked down the narrow gangway she lost all feeling of apprehension. She was aware of nothing and no-one, conscious only of the dress she was wearing and of the details she was supposed to show off. She pirouetted and stopped, then walked on again, head high, shoulders well back, glorious red-gold hair glinting as the spotlights gleamed on it. There was a burst of applause as she finished and her place was taken by another model. From then on, no-one had a chance to wonder what was happening, so busy were they changing, showing each dress and then tearing back to the dressing-room to slip into another one.

"How do you think it's going?" Sara panted, as she passed Mrs. Fielding in the doorway.

"Very well, I think," the vendeuse replied. "It was a little tricky at first because Marc's line was so new, but once the eye became accustomed to it, the women liked it. I think it'll be a success."

"I hope so," Sara said and hurried into the dressing-room.

Mrs. Fielding's hopes were justified for when the Collection came to its conclusion with Sara appearing as the Bride and the other models as her bridesmaids, there was a spontaneous burst of cheering from everyone in the audience. No need to wonder now what people thought. The Spring Collection was a triumph.

How great a triumph it was, was proved by the following morning's papers, for every fashion column extolled the new season's line as portrayed by Britain's most advanced couturier, Marc Donnell.

Sara glowed with pride as she scanned the paper on her way to work and she raced down Shepherd's Market and tore up the stairs of the salon eager to add her congratulations to those Marc had already received.

She had reached the corridor leading to his studio when Mrs. Fielding came after her, her face flushed, her demeanour agitated.

"Oh there you are, Sara, I've been watching out for you. Go and make yourself look presentable and then come into Marc's office."

"I was going there now."

"Well make yourself tidy first."

"Why? Who's there?"

Mrs. Fielding looked even more flustered. "Go *on* Sara, and stop arguing."

A few moments later, mystification warring with apprehension, Sara knocked on the door of his office and went in. To her surprise seated next to him was a petite, middle-aged woman wearing a stunningly smart suit that bespoke Paris. Atop her silver hair was perched a small flowered hat and Sara did not need anyone to tell her it came from New York. American women—no matter what the season or the occasion— had a penchant for tiny flowered hats!

"I—I'm sorry, Mr. Donnell," she stammered. "I didn't realise you were busy. I'll come back later."

"No, no, I want you now. I'd like you to meet Mrs. Marriott."

He stood up and as Sara came forward Mrs. Marriott smiled at her.

"Why, you're even prettier without your theatrical make-up."

Sara looked from the woman to Marc and he nodded. "Mrs. Marriott was at our Show yesterday. She owns Marriott's of Fifth Avenue."

Sara was suitably impressed for Marriott's was one of the leading American stores, and if Mrs. Marriott was here now it must mean she liked Marc's clothes. And if she liked them and bought them it would give him his first opening in the States. Her excitement must have shown in her face for the woman gave a gentle laugh.

"I can see Miss Gay is a fan of yours."

Sara stared at the American, surprised that she should know her name. Marc sat at his desk again and his fingers drummed on the top in a way that bespoke nervousness.

"Sit down, Sara," he said abruptly. "We—Mrs. Marriott that is, wants to talk to you."

"Oh no, you tell her Marc."

Marc hesitated. "You see, Sara, it's like this. Mrs. Marriott liked our Collection."

"I more than liked it," Mrs. Marriott intervened. "I thought it was absolutely fabulous. In fact, I've bought it all, lock, stock and barrel!"

Sara stared at her in wonder and the woman laughed again.

"Don't look so surprised, if I make up my mind

about something I go the whole way. And I've never been wrong yet! I want my store to be Marc's shop-window and so I want to show everything he produces. That includes *you*."

"Me?" Sara said. "I don't understand you."

"It's quite simple. You're Marc's top model and after watching you yesterday I understand why. His dresses are wonderful, but with you in them they become even more so. That's why, for his first Season in New York it's very important that he is given the best send-off. That's why I've made one stipulation before I sign my name to a cheque for his entire Collection."

Sara moistened her lips, knowing what was coming and yet unable to believe it could be so.

"And what—and what is that stipulation?" she stammered.

"That Marc Donnell releases you for three months so that you can come to New York with me and model his clothes!"

CHAPTER VI

ONCE the initial shock had worn off, Sara could hardly contain her delight. To go to New York for three months! It seemed unbelievable, yet it was true. Although reluctant to lose his favourite model for such a long period, Marc could see the justification of Mrs. Marriott's request and because he wanted his Collection to be a success realised he could not refuse it. All that was left to Sara was to obtain her parents' permission and try to find someone to share the flat with Beryl. In fact, it was the problem of Beryl that weighed most on her mind and she was still pondering on it when she returned to the flat that evening.

It was unthinkable for her friend to stay in London on her own and unthinkable to let her down since, had it not been for Sara, Beryl would never have come to London in the first place. She was so depressed by the thought of what she would have to say to her friend that she lost her appetite and toyed with the food on her plate until Beryl put down her fork in exasperation.

"What's the matter with you, Sara? Are you feeling off-colour?"

Knowing it could not be put off any longer, Sara recounted her interview with Mrs. Marriott and Beryl heard her out in silence, making no comment until she had come to the end.

"You're worrying what's going to happen to me in this flat, I suppose?"

"Yes. It isn't just the question of the rent—I could pay my share even when I'm in the States—but you know very well your parents wouldn't let you stay here alone and I'm sure you wouldn't want to either."

"No, I wouldn't," Beryl admitted. "But I don't think the problem arises. You see a girl who works at the office has been sharing a place with another girl who's just got married, and the other day she asked me if I'd like to share a flat with her. I told her I was living with you, but I'm sure she'd be delighted to come here for a few months until she finds another place of her own."

Sara's face cleared. "What a marvellous idea." All at once her appetite returned and she picked up her fork. The only thing left now was to obtain her parents' permission and she was sure that once they had met Mrs Marriott they would not withhold it.

In this Sara was proved right, for both her mother and father were charmed by Tina Marriott who arrived for lunch the following Sunday. By the time the American woman was due to return to London it had been decided that Sara would fly with her to the States in two weeks time.

"But there's so much to do," Sara murmured. "I doubt if I'll get it done."

"Put some American hustle into it," Mrs. Marriott

commanded. "I'm not leaving without you, so you'd better be ready."

Ready Sara was, although looking back on it she could hardly credit the amount she had had to do in such a short space of time. Not the least of her chores had been spending what seemed hours at the beautiful offices of the American Embassy at Grosvenor Square—a building so imposing that Sara's heart had quailed when she had first seen it. But the officials had been extremely helpful and within a week she had obtained her visa and working permit.

She spent her final week-end with her parents and was delighted when they invited Peter down as well. She would miss him while she was away, though watching his attentiveness to Beryl on the Saturday night, she realised with a pang that he would not miss her in quite the same way. It required an effort not to be jealous, and firmly she warned herself of being a dog in the manger. She and Peter were only friends; she had no right to object to his obvious liking for Beryl.

On the Sunday morning her mother and father decided to motor her direct to London Airport.

"It's such a long way away," Mrs. Gay murmured, voicing last-minute doubts. "If anything's wrong with you, cable us immediately."

"Nothing'll be wrong, Mummy," Sara replied. "America's a civilised country, you know. I'm not going to the backwoods."

"And don't come back with a Yankee accent either!" her brother piped up.

Sara tweaked his ear and he retaliated by trying to

knock off the jaunty little hat she was wearing.

"Sara! Tommy! Stop it." Mrs. Gay turned round in her seat to admonish them. "Honestly Sara, anyone would think you're a child!"

"She still is," her father remarked.

Realising there was some justification in what he had said, Sara gave her brother a severe look and settled back sedately in the corner.

Mrs. Marriott was waiting for her at London Airport, and together they walked over to the Pan-American ticket counter and handed in their reservations. Their luggage was weighed, and Sara looked anxiously at the clock hoping it was not overweight. Luckily she had a couple of pounds to spare, although to her surprise Mrs. Marriott's was more than twenty pounds overweight.

"I'm afraid I'll have to charge you for excess luggage," the official remarked.

Mrs. Marriott handed him a cheque for what seemed a staggeringly large amount and Sara could not help remarking upon it.

Mrs. Marriott shrugged. "One of the disadvantages of travelling by air is that one's luggage is always overweight. I half expected yours would be too."

"I didn't dare," Sara confessed. "As it is, I've skimped terribly on my clothes."

"Never mind. You'll be able to buy lots of nice ones in the States. If you behave like most of your compatriots who work in our country I guess you'll put half your salary on your back!"

"I want to save some," Sara said firmly. "At least a quarter."

"That will still give you a fair amount to squander! Your pay will be much higher than you've earned here. A hundred dollars a week."

Sara gasped. "But that's over thirty pounds!"

"You'll earn every penny of it," came the reply. "And anyway the cost of living is much higher in New York."

"It still seems like a fortune."

Mrs. Marriott's reply was forestalled by their flight number being called over the loudspeaker, and Sara bade her parents a tearful goodbye before following her new employer into the Customs Hall. Examination of their luggage was extremely cursory, as were the questions asked them by the Currency Officer, and within a few minutes they were ushered into the Departure Lounge, which was half-full of people. There was a counter for those anxious to buy last-minute souvenirs of England: tartan rugs, cashmere sweaters and china, while the bookstall displayed the latest magazines and books.

Soon she heard their flight number called again and she followed the rest of the passengers outside. To her surprise she was ushered into a single-decker bus, and Mrs. Marriott explained that because jet aircraft needed an extremely long runway both for take-off and landing, they were being driven to the outer perimeter of the Airport where their plane was waiting for them.

"I've never been in a jet before," Sara murmured. "I'm rather scared."

"There's nothing to be scared of," Mrs. Marriott remarked. "You'll see."

Sara certainly did see. The jet was so large that it seemed to her inexperienced eye that no power on earth could be sufficient to make it leave the ground! Inside it appeared even larger and she settled back in a padded armchair and tied the safety belt around her. Nervously she clenched her hands, half hearing the soft music coming through the loudspeakers placed over each seat. She was travelling first class, a luxury at which she had demurred, but to which Mrs. Marriott had insisted on treating her, saying she wanted the pleasure of Sara's company during the six-hour flight.

Soon everyone had settled down, the doors were closed and the aircraft taxied along the runway. Expecting to hear a deafening roar from the engines as they revved up for take-off, she was astonished when she felt the plane zoom forward and, looking out of the window, saw they were airborne. She looked at Mrs. Marriott in astonishment and the woman nudged her elbow and pointed to the window again. Sara looked out once more, her astonishment increasing as she saw that they were already thousands of feet in the air! They must have soared upwards in an almost vertical climb.

London was obliterated beneath clouds and above them the sun sparkled, sun which Sara had not seen so clearly for months.

"I didn't want you to miss it," Mrs. Marriott said in her ear. "Take-off in a jet is quite different from any other aircraft. You just soar up like a bird."

"You certainly do," Sara said, and settled back in her chair with a sigh of relief.

The time was ten a.m. and they were due to arrive at Idlewild Airport in New York at four o'clock Greenwich Meantime, which was eleven o'clock American time. That meant she would have the whole day to settle in the hostel which Mrs. Marriott had booked for her.

A hostel again. She wondered whether it would be different from the London one, whether the rules would be as strict, the curfew as limited. But she did not like to question Mrs. Marriott in case the woman thought she was being critical and decided to wait and see what the position was herself. After all, with a salary of a hundred dollars a week she might even be able to afford a flat!

The journey passed quickly. There were magazines to read, fabulous food to eat and champagne to drink. Sara had only tasted champagne once before—when she had modelled clothes in Monte Carlo—but she sipped a glass now, enjoying the sensation of bubbles that tickled her nose and the feeling of exhilaration it engendered.

"To tell the truth I'm generally a tomato juice girl," she confessed.

"And very wise too. Drink is unnecessary and harmful. When you get to my age you might feel the need for a pick-me-up, but not otherwise."

During the flight, which was so smooth that Sara could not believe they were flying forty thousand feet above sea level, Mrs. Marriott told her something about the store and where she lived.

"We keep open from nine till six every day except Saturday, when we close at one. But on Monday and

Thursday we're open till nine p.m. That gives the working girl a chance to get some shopping done without forgoing her lunch hour."

"Very nice for the shopper," Sara murmured, "but pretty hard on the assistants!"

"They all get corresponding time off," Mrs. Marriott answered. "But generally we work harder in the States than you do in Europe. I'm in my office myself every morning at nine sharp."

"Do you live in the city?"

"During the week only. I have an apartment overlooking the East River."

"Is that rather like Chelsea and the Thames?" Sara asked.

"In a way." Mrs. Marriott looked amused. "At one time it was most depressing, with factories and old buildings, but now there are wonderful skyscrapers going up and it's very much in demand. I like it because of the view of the water. I'm fond of the sea."

"So am I. That's why I love going to Frimpton for my week-ends."

"If you like the sea you must come and spend a week-end with me at my house on Long Island. It'll do the place good to have a young person in it again."

Sara noticed the use of the word "again" and wondered whether Mrs. Marriott had any children, but as the woman did not refer to any she did not like to question her.

Promptly at two o'clock they were requested to fasten their seat belts again, and as they did so the plane began to lose height. It was a much more un-

comfortable sensation to go down than it had been to
go up, for the descent was slower and accompanied
by unpleasant bumps. Sara was considerably relieved
when they broke through the cloud and she saw land
beneath her: rolling fields, clusters of houses, and to
one side the sea. Because there were two more aircraft waiting to land they were forced to circle for
about fifteen minutes, but at last they received the
signal and the plane made the final drop towards the
runway. Sara breathed a sigh of relief when she felt
the wheels touch the ground, and she swallowed hard
as her eardrums throbbed. The most remarkable
thing about the journey was the lack of noise, but
even so she felt a dizzy sensation in her head and
asked Mrs. Marriott how long it would last.

"A couple of hours. But this is much better than
going on a boat. Last time I travelled on the Queen
Elizabeth I walked with a list for three days after
I landed!"

Giggling, Sara followed the woman down the gangway of the aircraft.

The American Customs were by no means as pleasant as their English counterparts and she was astonished that every single bag was opened and carefully examined. They seemed to be particularly vigi-
lant with their own compatriots, and though Sara's
luggage was opened it only received a cursory search.
When they finally left the Customs behind there was
a further investigation by the immigration authorities,
but eventually all the formalities were completed and
they went outside the Airport where they were met by
a negro chauffeur who stood beside the longest, shin-

iest car Sara had ever seen. It was a caramel coloured
Cadillac, with cream and caramel upholstery.

Sara took her place beside Mrs. Marriott and they
glided towards the city. It was a long drive and she
looked around with interest, noticing the strangeness
of the houses which appeared to incorporate a great
deal of wood and glass. Even the trees were different,
and though denuded of leaves, for Winter was still
with them, seemed taller and larger.

But the difference that she noticed outside New
York was nothing compared with the difference she
noticed once they were in the city itself. The skyscrapers loomed above her head almost blotting out
the sight of the sky, the roads were straight and at
each intersection there were lights, which made progress down Fifth Avenue a jerky affair.

"You won't find it easy to get lost in New York,"
Mrs. Marriott explained. "Our streets have numbers
instead of names, and if you want Forty-Second Street
or Fifty-Seventh Street you just have to count! The
only streets that have names are ones that go at right
angles like Fifth Avenue, Madison Avenue, Park
Avenue and a few more."

"What a marvellous idea," Sara commented. "Not a
bit like London."

"You're telling me! I spent an hour wandering
around before I found Marc Donnell's salon . . . . I've
a thing about using taxis when I'm abroad. I always
go on a bus if I can—it helps one to get the feeling of
a city."

The car swung left and stopped outside a tall, grey
building.

"This is your hostel," Mrs. Marriott said. "I managed to get you a room on your own, and I hope you'll like it."

"I'm sure I shall," Sara said, and watched as the chauffeur carried her case up the steps. Then she bent forward and peered into the car. "I'll be at Marriott's at nine a.m. sharp," she promised.

"Good. Then I can introduce you to Gina Banks. She's in charge of the fashion department, and while you're in the store you'll be under her aegis."

There was such a look of dismay on Sara's face that Mrs. Marriott smiled.

"Don't look so upset. You'll like Gina. She's far less autocratic than I am."

"I don't think you're a bit autocratic," Sara said impulsively. "I think you're wonderful."

"What a sweet thing to say. Now go to your room and have a rest. I'll leave you to settle in on your own and maybe do a bit of exploring. Bye-bye, Sally dear and—" she caught her breath. "I mean . . . . Sara. Bye-bye."

Quickly she leaned back in her seat and the car glided away from the kerb. Sara watched until it disappeared from sight before mounting the steps of the hostel, a frown on her face.

Why had Mrs. Marriott called her Sally instead of Sara? She did not think it had been a slip of the tongue but a momentary forgetfulness. Yet the woman had not spoken of anyone called Sally, neither had she mentioned having a daughter of that name. Yet from the stricken look on Mrs. Marriott's face when the name had slipped out, Sara was convinced that Sally meant something special in her life.

"Interesting," she thought to herself as she pushed open the door and went into the hostel. "Sally X. I wonder who she really is."

CHAPTER VII

MORE quickly than she had believed possible, Sara settled down to working in the big department store. Everyone went out of their way to be helpful, especially Gina Banks, the head of the fashion department, who was a bustling, efficient woman, the epitome of New York glamour. She had been a model at one time and consequently took a great interest in Sara, anxious to know all about her training at the Lena Lane Model School, and what it was like to work with Marc Donnell, for whom she had great admiration.

The store employed three other models though Sara did not come into much contact with them, for Marc's clothes were shown in an ante-room off the main floor. A fact which she understood when she saw the difference in price between ready-to-wear clothes and custom-made ones.

"Labour is terribly expensive here," Gina Banks explained. "You can buy a mass-produced dress—a lovely one too—for as little as fifteen dollars, which is about five pounds in your money, whereas if you want something made especially for you you'll have to pay anything from a hundred dollars upwards."

"I'll stick to ready-mades," Sara grinned. "Though your 'finish' isn't as good as ours, your styling is much better."

"Cheap dresses aren't made to last," the older woman said. "Girls here buy dresses for one season only—and they buy lots of them."

Sara realised the truth of this on her first Thursday evening on duty. During the late opening night a different clientèle came into the store, girls of her own age with limited money to spend, and it was astonishing to see the amount they laid out for clothes and the casualness with which they bought not one or two but sometimes even three dresses!

Sara's duties, although they necessitated longer hours, were not arduous. In the morning, after she had clocked in, she would take the lift to the seventh floor, take off her outdoor clothes and slip into any one of the Teen and Twenty Collection she fancied. Then, in her elegant Donnell dress, she was at liberty to wander into any other department, provided there was no-one down in the Appointment Book for whom she had to model.

Occasionally customers came in to see the whole Collection and when this happened Sara felt she should have taken a course in being a quick-change artiste, for she had to tumble from one dress into another, always careful to wear the correct accessories with each one.

During her first week Mrs. Marriott invited more than a hundred fashion writers to have cocktails with her and view Marc Donnell's clothes, and she engaged two other models to help. Sara might have been the

star pupil at the Lena Lane School, but the New York
models took her breath away by their elegance and
grooming. And how thin they were! Wraith-like crea-
tures who looked as if a breath of wind would blow
them away. For their part, they found Sara equally
intriguing, admiring the spontaneity with which she
showed the clothes and her general air of youthful-
ness. They also commented on her figure, and said that
were she to put her name down on the books of any
well-known Agency, she would be asked to lose at
least ten pounds!

"I'm five feet seven inches," Sara said, "and my
measurements are 36, 23, 36. If I lost ten pounds I'd
look like a skeleton!"

Although she found it enjoyable to work with
American models, Sara preferred being on her own,
for then she could wander around the store to her
heart's delight, and listen to conversations between
customer and assistant. As the days passed England
receded, and it seemed as though she had always lived
in New York and always worked at Marriott's.

The city itself was a constant source of delight. She
was intrigued by the single-decker buses with their
weird machine in the front for collecting fares; she
was delighted by the self-service cafés, the hambur-
ger shops serving delicious sandwiches of all types,
and the automats where food was displayed in little
glass compartments that opened at the insertion of a
coin. But best of all, she loved to wander down Fifth
Avenue itself and look in the windows which seemed
like lighted Aladdin's caves, so strange and wonderful
was the collection of articles for sale. Every other shop

seemed to be selling costume jewellery—and what jewellery it was! Never had she seen artificial pearls and diamonds that looked so real!

It was not until Sara had been working at Marriott's for two weeks that she learned the identity of the Sally to whom Mrs. Marriott had referred. She had decided to forgo her usual lunch and instead, armed with sandwiches and fruit, was taking a stroll in Central Park when she saw Gina Banks sitting on a bench, her face upturned to the sun. Sara was not sure whether to walk past, but the woman tilted her head and saw her.

"Hi Sara. You're doing what I like to do—eat out of doors instead of inside."

"It seemed such a lovely day," Sara confessed. "Back home March is always frightfully windy and cold."

"It's generally like that here. I guess we're having an Indian spring instead of an Indian summer!"

Sara sat down and began to munch a sandwich. "Can I offer you something?"

"Not for me, honey. This is my dieting day. That's why I'm here." She rummaged in her handbag and took out a cigarette. "How do you like working with us?" she asked, as she blew out a cloud of smoke, careful to avoid Sara's sandwiches.

"I love it. It's much easier than I thought, and the girls are very nice too. They don't seem a bit jealous."

"Why should they be jealous of you?" Mrs. Banks asked, surprised.

Sara shrugged. "Back home the girls in the hostel always envied me my job. But here they don't seem to care. I mean they're curious about what I do but that's all."

"Curiosity instead of envy," Gina Banks murmured. "Yes, I know what you mean. But don't think we Americans are nicer people just because we aren't jealous. You see, we all believe that given the right opportunity we can get to the top too. In other words, everybody can rise to be the President, if they really put their hearts into it!"

Sara laughed. "And that's another difference I like. You're all so wonderfully ambitious. In England ambition is something that's frowned on—especially if you're a girl. I'm making us sound frightfully old-fashioned but . . . . do you know what I mean?"

"I think so. Over here no parent would stand in their daughter's way if she wanted to get a job in Timbuctoo, but I'm pretty sure your parents thought twice about letting you move from your seaside town to London."

"However did you know!" Sara exclaimed. Then as she saw Mrs. Banks' expression she started to giggle. "Have you ever been to England?

"No, but I'm hoping to go in the fall—the Autumn, I mean. Mrs. Marriott goes over every six months and I'm trying to persuade her not to do the second trip this year, but to let me go instead. She hasn't been well lately and we all think she should take it easy."

"She seems full of energy," Sara said in surprise.

"She isn't the sort of woman who panders to herself. Anyway, it isn't so much a physical illness as a mental one. Since Sally left she's been getting dreadful headaches and—"

Mrs. Banks stopped in confusion but Sara's curiosity got the better of her discretion.

"Is Sally her daughter?"

"Yes."

"I thought so. Mrs. Marriott and I flew here together and when she dropped me at the hostel and said goodbye, she called me Sally instead of Sara. I had a feeling it was more than just a slip of the tongue."

"It certainly was," came the reply. "You're very much like Sally, you know. In fact, when I first saw you I nearly had a fit because you could have been her twin!"

Suddenly many things fell into place in Sara's mind: Mrs. Marriott's friendliness towards her, her insistence that she and she alone should come to New York, the way in which she had paid for her to travel first class and used her influence to instal her in one of the most exclusive girls' hostels in New York.

"What happened to Mrs. Marriott's daughter?" she asked. "Is she dead?"

"Oh no. She—she left home. She quarrelled with her mother and . . . ."

Mrs. Banks' pale blue eyes looked at Sara speculatively and then, as if making up her mind that the girl could be trusted, she said:

"I'll tell you the whole story if you promise not to mention it to anyone, and certainly not to tell Mrs. Marriott you know about it."

Sara nodded and the woman spoke again.

"To understand Mrs. Marriott's feelings about her daughter you have to understand Mrs. Marriott herself. She was left a widow after only a few years of married life and found herself almost penniless with a young child to bring up. Her husband's family had a great deal of money but they never approved of their son marrying Tina Marriott, and so when Ralph died they wiped their hands of her."

"Like Georgina Howard," Sara said involuntarily. "She's a vendeuse at Donnell's."

Mrs. Banks nodded. "Well, as I was saying, all those factors made Tina Marriott determined to give her daughter the very best of everything. *She'd* show her in-laws that she didn't give a darn about them! And in order to do it she worked non-stop eighteen hours a day for three years. She'd always been interested in fashion, and after starting work in a small dress shop she ended up owning it! Working so hard meant she didn't have much home life though, and she wasn't as close to Sally as she'd have wished. She tried to compensate by giving her everything she wanted—materially—and I'm afraid she spoilt her dreadfully." Mrs. Banks ground her cigarette beneath her heel. "Well, she grew up to be a very pretty, high-spirited girl, interested in art and painting. Her mother sent her to Art School and that's when the trouble began. Sally fell in love with a painter there, a young man her mother didn't approve of. She and Sally quarrelled bitterly and the girl ran off to get married."

"And she hasn't been home since?"

"No. I don't know exactly what happened between them but—well, I gather Sally hurt her mother terribly. She accused her of leaving her in the care of nannies and governesses, and only bothering with her when she wanted to live a life of her own."

"There was some justification in that, wasn't there," Sara commented, "Though I'd have thought Sally would have realised why her mother behaved the way she did."

"Young people don't always realise these things. *You* only see it because you're looking at the situation from a distance. If it had been your own mother you might also have felt unloved and unwanted. Not that Sally had any right to feel unwanted. You've no idea the money Mrs. Marriott spent on her."

"And where's Sally now?"

"No-one knows. I asked Mrs. Marriott once, but she doesn't like talking about it. I think she regrets the quarrel but she's got too much pride to go and find her —even if she knew where to look."

"It doesn't seem right for a mother and daughter not to speak to one another any more. Why didn't Mrs. Marriott want her to marry?"

"Because the young man didn't have a job, because he was—to use your phraseology—a beatnik!"

Sara could not help smiling as she tried to imagine the elegant, poised Mrs. Marriott with a beatnik son-in-law. Yet visualising the sort of life Sally must have led, the nannies and governesses, the careful upbringing, she could easily see why a beatnik would appeal to her. If only her mother had seen it too!

"Wouldn't it be marvellous if they could make it up?" she murmured.

"You're forgetting the husband," Mrs. Banks said drily. "No matter how much Mrs. Marriott loves her daughter, I can't see her accepting a ne'er-do-well as a son-in-law. You see, she was pretty certain he was marrying Sally for her money, and Sally would have had a lot of it if she'd married with her mother's approval."

"I don't believe that a boy who's a painter and a beatnik could be interested in money! I mean, the two things don't go together."

"I suppose not. Not that I've ever thought about it before." The pale blue eyes were warm as they rested on the girl in front of her. "I think there's quite a bit of logic in what you've just said. What a pity you weren't here a few years ago. Maybe if you had been, this quarrel would never have happened. But it's too late now. I don't think Mrs Marriott will ever speak to her daughter again."

When Sara returned to the store she could not forget Mrs. Banks' last words, for they seemed so unnatural and cruel. How could a mother cut her daughter out of her life? Words said in temper were rarely adhered to once the temper had abated. Proud Mrs. Marriott might be, and obstinate too, but certainly not unloving.

"If only there was something I could do," she thought.

But of course, before she could do anything, she had to find Sally. And to find a girl whom she had never seen before and whose married name she did not even know seemed such an impossible task that she tried to push it out of her mind.

CHAPTER VIII

SARA did not have the opportunity, since she was working so hard, to make many friends other than with the girls whom she met at the hostel. Occasionally she would go out with one or the other of them to the cinema—which they called the movies—or to one of the many down-town restaurants where they would sample Chinese food, Russian food, Hungarian food and on one occasion, Hawaiian!

No matter what one said about New York, it was certainly cosmopolitan, and as the days passed Sara felt a widening of her horizons, a broadening of her outlook that gave her a greater feeling of confidence. England seemed a long way away and her life with Beryl a dull one. Not that she was doing anything exciting here; it was merely the difference in atmosphere, the very electricity in the air which made one feel invigorated and alive. Intensely alive!

One Sunday morning she was lying in bed in her small room, staring through the window at the white clouds chasing one another across the sky, when one of the girls knocked on her door and told her she was wanted on the telephone.

Putting on her dressing gown and slippers she hurried down the hall to the telephone at the far end. How unlike the British hostel this one was. There had only been one telephone there and that had been placed in the most draughty corner of the entrance lobby. Here each floor had a telephone, complete with table, chair, pencil and pad for taking down notes!

She wondered who could be calling her, and was intensely surprised to hear Mrs. Marriott's voice at the other end inviting her over for lunch.

"I didn't go out to Long Island this week-end," she explained. "I was working late at the store yesterday and felt it wasn't worth travelling out there just for one day. So as I'm in town it seemed a good opportunity to have you over for a chat." For a moment the voice lost its authority and became hesitant. "If you haven't made any other arrangements, that is. A pretty girl like you is bound to have—"

"I've no other plans," Sara said quickly. "I'd love to come over and see you."

"Good. I'll expect you at twelve-thirty."

Sara dressed for her luncheon with great care, and as she left the hostel knew she was looking her best in a full-skirted navy suit, the pleats swinging around her shapely legs, the short bolero cut to disclose her tiny waist. Many were the glances turned in her direction and many the whistles she received. How unlike England where one could walk down the road looking as glamorous as the Queen of Sheba and arouse no more excitement than if one were a grandmother taking a dog for a stroll!

She was smiling at the thought when she reached

the address Mrs. Marriott had given her and found herself in front of an imposing block of flats. A blue and gold canopy spread out over the pavement and a commissionaire guarded the plate glass entrance doors. He held them open as Sara walked forward and realising she was a stranger, asked her where she wanted to go. When she told him, he smiled.

"Take the elevator at the bottom of the stairs and go straight to the top."

Thanking him she entered the lobby. The air was heavy with heat and miniature palm trees stood in golden urns beside velvet settees, while oyster satin swathed the walls. Even the lift looked like an Arabian tent, though when she pressed the button she was zoomed sky-wards at a pace that no Eastern potentate would have allowed!

When she stepped out on to the top floor only one door faced her and with awe she realised that Mrs. Marriott's penthouse occupied the whole area. As if someone inside the flat had heard the lift ascend, the door opened and a coloured maid in a black silk uniform ushered her in, took her outdoor things and then led her into the drawing-room where Mrs. Marriott was seated.

Sara stopped on the threshold unable to believe in the splendour that met her gaze. Silk Persian rugs in blue and scarlet and gold lay on the gleaming parquet floor, their colour picked out in the magnificent paintings that lined three walls. The fourth wall was given over entirely to a picture window and as she advanced further into the room she glimpsed a breathtaking view of the New York skyline. Mrs. Marriott followed her glance and after greeting her warmly, led her on to the terrace where hydrangeas bloomed in gaily coloured tubs and wickerwork chairs invited them to sit down. Sara walked to the edge of the terrace and saw the Hudson River far below. She saw also the graceful bridges spanning the water and the long lines of cars—those inevitable cars—that always seemed to be speeding in and out of the city.

"How small it makes one feel to look at things from such a height," she murmured.

"It either makes you feel small or big," Mrs. Marriott said surprisingly. "It depends on your temperament. Personally I feel as though I'm master of all I survey when I stand up here and look down on the city."

Sara made no comment on these words, though she wondered how true they were.

They returned to the drawing-room and remembering she did not drink Mrs. Marriott gave her a tomato juice and handed her some delicious canapés: paté on toast, caviare with chopped egg and onion, and bowls of nuts.

While Sara was sipping her drink, her hostess asked her how she had settled down in New York, and nervously at first, but with growing confidence, Sara told her all she had done since they had last met.

Occasionally Mrs. Marriott laughed at something Sara said, and as the girl relaxed she lost her shyness, her conversation becoming less inhibited as she gave a vivid account of her life in the store and her explorations of the city in the evenings and week-ends.

Lunch was served in a room as magnificent as the

one they had left behind. One wall was occupied by
a tropical aquarium and while Sara ate delicious ome-
lette and chicken soufflé she watched angel fish glid-
ing gracefully backwards and forwards across the
blue-green water.

Immediately lunch was over she stood up to go,
unwilling to overstay her welcome, but to her surprise Mrs. Marriott, after ascertaining that Sara had
no other plans for the day, begged her to stay and keep
her company.

"I'm not doing anything either, except maybe
watch a television show, and if you wouldn't find it
too boring to stay with me. . . ."

"I'd love nothing better," Sara said eagerly. "You've
no idea how wonderful it is for me to be here. Living
in the hostel's fine but this—why, I feel like a film
star!"

Mrs. Marriott laughed. "I like your enthusiasm,
Sara. But I'm sure you've seen lovelier homes than
this."

"Never. My parents have a very small house. Why,
the whole of it would go into your drawing-room."

"This is nothing," the woman shrugged. "You
should see my place out on Long Island. I'm very
proud of that. I love collecting antiques and pictures,
and all my best things are out there. You must come
and spend a week-end with me if you're not too busy."

"I'd never be too busy," Sara said. Then afraid that
she had sounded too eager, blushed and looked at the
floor.

The rest of the day sped by, and when Sara looked
out of the window again she saw that dusk had fallen

and that the city lay in front of her like a glittering diamond necklace.

"Now I really have outstayed my welcome," she said. "Honestly, Mrs. Marriott you must be tired of hearing me talk on and on."

"I've loved every minute of it. I see many people during the week, as you know, but when the week-end comes round I either go out to Long Island or stay here by myself. I'm jealous of my spare time, and I only invite people to share it if I like them. You're one who is always welcome."

"That's the nicest thing anybody's ever said to me."

"I'm sure lots of people have said nice things to you, Sara."

"Well, maybe people of my own age. But not—not important people like you."

Mrs. Marriott laughed. "What a child you are. Sometimes you seem much older than your age and then—like now—you seem so young and unspoiled." She stood up, the folds of her long housecoat falling gracefully around her. "Please don't go yet. My cook always goes out on Sunday evenings and my maid doesn't sleep in, so I'm alone in the apartment. If you like we can hustle up something for supper, bring it in on a tray and watch television."

"That sounds wonderful," Sara said. "You've no idea how I've been longing to get my hands on a gas-stove since I arrived in New York. That's one thing I miss in the hostel."

"Well, tonight you can cook to your heart's content."

Mrs. Marriott led her into a kitchen that was the

last word in modernity. A deep freeze, a refrigerator, a washing machine, a dish-washer, and two eye-level ovens.

"It makes human beings seem unnecessary," Sara giggled, and gasped as Mrs. Marriott opened the refrigerator door and she saw shelves stacked with food.

"Take your choice," Mrs. Marriott said. "I can't even boil water without burning it, so I'll leave everything to you."

"You don't have to cook," Sara said. "You're so capable at other things."

As she spoke she took out some food and put it on the table, trying to remember the last meal she'd had with Marc. She looked in the refrigerator. Yes, there was a small joint of meat. She took it out and stared at it. Luck was with her, for it was lamb. Now if only she could remember the flavourings Marc had used she might be able to produce something that would not shame her in Mrs. Marriott's eyes. Humming gaily as she worked, Sara started to prepare a casserole of lamb, adding herbs and spices and a dash of wine. Within half an hour there was a pungent aroma in the kitchen and Mrs. Marriott, perched like a girl on the edge of the table, watched Sara ladle out two platefuls of stew.

"I didn't have any of this in mind," she admitted, as they carried their respective trays back into the living-room. "I just thought we would have egg on toast."

By now Sara was too at home to feel shy. "It isn't good for you just to have egg on toast. I'm sure you don't eat proper meals during the week when you're working, and it's good for you to tuck in during the week-end."

Mrs. Marriott giggled, and Sara had the feeling that never before—or certainly not in a long while—had the woman been teased in this way. Calm and understanding though she was, Mrs. Marriott was an autocrat and the people who worked with her treated her with respect tinged with fear. "Yet I'm not afraid of her," Sara thought as she sat on a pouffe in front of the television set. "Why, she could easily be my mother."

Something of what was passing through her mind must have been telepathically communicated to Mrs. Marriott, for the smile suddenly seemed to leave the woman's face and there was a look of such sadness on it that tears filled Sara's eyes.

"It's been so lovely having you here," Mrs. Marriott said. "For the first time in—oh, a long while—this penthouse feels like home. I'm going to ask you something, Sara, but you can refuse if you want to. I won't mind."

There was a long pause and Sara put down her plate. Her mouth was dry and nervously she rubbed her tongue over her lips. She did not know what was coming, yet she sensed the turmoil in her hostess.

"Yes," she said. "What is it?"

"Would you—would you be prepared to leave the hostel and come and live here with me?"

CHAPTER IX

SARA'S delight at being offered the chance to live in such a beautiful home was tinged with fear that one day Mrs. Marriott might regret her generous offer. But as the days passed and Sara settled into the penthouse, she and her employer established a rapport that made it impossible for either of them to believe they had not lived together for years.

One night as she lay in bed, and heard far below her the constant hum of traffic, she wondered exactly why she should feel so at home with Mrs. Marriott— as at home as she felt with her own mother. And yet, if she were really honest she would have to admit that with Mrs. Marriott she felt even *more* at home. Mrs. Gay had always tried to understand her daughter but as Sara's career blossomed, so the gulf between them began to widen. Clothes to Mrs. Gay meant a sensible navy suit, a print summer dress and a couple of cotton ones, while the mention of the word glamour conjured up pictures of painted hussies. Sara knew none of this was true yet how could she explain it? With Mrs. Marriott there was was no need for explanation because fashion and glamour were part of her everyday existence.

Within a few days of moving into the penthouse the two women had established a routine together. Unwilling for anyone at the store to know where she was living in case they thought she was doing it to curry favour—Sara expressed the desire to arrive at the store on her own and refused the offer of a lift in the Cadillac. It meant a brisk walk down Fifth Avenue for twenty blocks, or else to be pushed and jostled in one of the over-crowded buses. But she preferred it that way, and though within a week the grapevine had informed everyone that Sara was, in actual fact, living at the penthouse, no-one made any unkind remarks about it.

As Spring approached she was working harder than ever for many debutantes came in to view the Collection. Debutantes, Sara decided, were the same the world over: just as silly and just as pampered! She had always believed there to be no class consciousness in the States, but she learnt this was far from the truth and that the élite Four Hundred were even more snobbish than their Society counterparts in Britain. Not that the bulk of the American people worried about the Four Hundred set, Sara discovered, and indeed Mrs. Marriott wryly informed her that some of the wealthiest people in the country did not appear between the illustrious pages of the American "Who's Who".

"In fact some of our wealthiest people insist on remaining *out* of it because they don't agree with all its snobbish implications."

But it was snobbish implications that made the young New York debutantes eager to wear Marc Don-

nell clothes, made them eager to wear French ones too
and Sara was rather amused to see some of Paul
Gerard's dresses on display. How long ago it seemed
since Marc had shown his Collection at Monte
Carlo!

Sara told her employer all that had happened on
that exciting visit and Mrs. Marriott listened keenly.

"You're fond of Marc Donnell, aren't you?"

"Yes."

They were sitting together in the penthouse, spending a quiet evening at home which Mrs Marriott had
done increasingly since Sara had moved in with her.
In fact, now Mrs. Marriott had someone to come home
to she was increasingly reluctant to accept social en-
gagements and on the few times when it was strictly
necessary had insisted on taking Sara with her. In
some ways Sara was convinced her employer was trying to put her in the place of her own daughter and
she wondered whether this was a good sign or not. It
certainly meant that the gap left by Sally Marriott
was still there and needed to be replaced.

"But I can never fill it," she thought. "Only her
daughter can do that."

The more she got to know Mrs. Marriott the more
she liked her. Not that she was an easy woman to get
on with—on the contrary she could be extremely ob-
durate, but on the other hand she had achieved won-
ders on her own and had reached an unrivalled position in the world of fashion.

"It must be a great strain running your store," she
said involuntarily.

Mrs. Marriott, busy with thoughts of Marc Donnell,

seemed surprised by the sudden change of conversation, but she nodded her head.

"It is. But I wouldn't change it for the world. As a matter of fact I'm thinking of opening another one. Out on Long Island. Most of the New York department stores have branches there now and I feel I've got to follow suit."

"But it would be much more work for you."

"Not really. All it will mean is that I'll buy twice as much. Instead of one Donnell Collection, I'll have two! No, the bulk of the work will be planning the building and the decor. Once that's done my main task will be over."

Sara leaned forward, her grey-green eyes shining. "It must be fun designing a building. Architecture's like fashion, isn't it? Except that with fashion your materials are fabrics, and with architecture it's bricks and stone."

"And a thousand and one other things too!" the woman laughed. "You're forgetting all your plastics!" As she spoke, she walked over to a French escritoire and from one of the drawers withdrew a sheet of paper which she held out to Sara.

Sara took it and saw a drawing of a large store. Mrs. Marriott's plans were obviously much more than mental ones for here was concrete proof that she meant to go ahead.

"The building should be finished in six months' time. I must have it ready before the Winter."

"I wish I could be here to see it, it looks wonderful."

"It will be wonderful." The silver head tilted. "And you could be here if you wanted to, Sara. There's no

need for you to go back to England. I'd be delighted
for you to work at Marriott's as long as you wish. In
fact, you needn't work if you don't want to. You can
stay on here and—and live with me."

Sara was speechless. She was intelligent enough to
know Mrs. Marriott liked her, but never in her wildest
imaginings had she anticipated such an offer being
made.

"It's very kind of you," she stammered, "but I
couldn't—I couldn't dream of it. I love my work and
I want to get to the top."

"There's no reason why you can't go on being a
model in New York. You'd get to the top much more
quickly."

"But England is my home and my family are there."

The mention of the word family caused Mrs. Marriott's face to tighten with pain and Sara leaned forward and kissed the lined cheek.

"Please don't look like that. I'm very happy here
with you and I hate the thought of having to leave,
but—but well, this isn't my home and I'm not—" she
hesitated and then took the plunge. "I'm not and never
could be your daughter."

"What do you know about my daughter?" Mrs.
Marriott said sharply.

Sara felt the colour drain from her face and wondered whether she should tell the truth. To do so
would implicate Gina Banks and she decided to be
evasive.

"Somebody mentioned it a little while ago. They
didn't say much—just that you had a daughter."

There was a long silence, a silence so tense that

Sara could hear every sound in the room. The ticking of the French clock on the marble mantelpiece, the creak of furniture, the sighing of the wind on the terrace outside.

"Yes, I did have a daughter," Mrs. Marriott said suddenly. "But as far as I'm concerned she no longer exists."

"You can't mean that!"

"How do *you* know what I mean? You don't know what Sally did to me. She broke my heart. Broke my heart, I tell you."

"And what did you do to *her?*" The moment the words were out, Sara longed to withdraw them, but it was too late and they echoed across the room like an accusation.

"What did I do to *her?*" Mrs. Marriott asked in surprise. "What do you mean?"

"Just that one person doesn't hurt another without being impelled to do so. Didn't you do something to your daughter that made her want to hurt you?"

"I forbade her to marry a penniless fortune-hunter! I warned her that if she ignored my advice I'd never see her again. Well, she did ignore my advice and she walked out and left me."

"How long ago was that?"

"Two years. And I've never heard from her since."

"Do you regret it?"

Sara asked the question not expecting an answer and she was aghast when Mrs. Marriott buried her head in her hands, her body shaken with sobs. Uncomfortably Sara wondered whether she should leave her alone, but when she made a move to get up the woman held on to her hand and she sank back on the settee and waited. After a little while Mrs. Marriott looked up, and though her eyes were red, her face was composed.

"Regret is an emotion I have never allowed myself. In fact, until you came on the scene I had almost convinced myself I'd cut Sally out of my heart as well as my life. But being with you and getting to know you has made a difference to my life. You're the sort of girl Sally could have been if I'd been able to devote more time to her. I see now only too clearly where I went wrong. I put work first. Yet it wasn't of myself I was thinking when I spent all those hours in the store —it was for Sally I did it, for Sally that I wanted to earn money and be successful. But by the time I *was* successful my relationship with my daughter was non-existent and there was no love between us."

"If there was no love between you, you wouldn't have felt so deeply about her."

"Well, maybe *I* loved her, but I don't think she felt anything for me. She was too spoilt and selfish to feel anything for *anybody!*"

"I'm sure that isn't true," Sara said. "I don't see how any girl who's spoiled and selfish could give up all this luxury and run away with a penniless man. After all, what can she be living on now?"

Mrs. Marriott looked surprised. "Do you know I never thought of that, and heaven knows I've thought about Sally until my head ached. You've got a good point there. If she really did marry Garry, she must be having a pretty hard time of it."

"Garry? Was that his name?"

"Yes." As if afraid she had given too much away, Mrs. Marriott said no more and Sara, realising that to continue the subject would be an unwelcome intrusion, changed the subject.

But as she lay in bed that night she mulled over the conversation. The more she thought about Sally, the more convinced she became that her assessment of the girl was right. No matter how selfish she might have been, no matter how much she had taken for granted the luxury her mother had heaped on her, if she had really married Garry and been with him over the past two years then she had surely learned, in the best possible way, all the pleasure that money could buy and all the bitterness that ensued when one did not have enough of it?

If only she could find the girl and bring mother and daughter together! She wondered whether Mrs. Marriott had made any attempt to do so and vowed that at the next opportunity she would try to find out.

The opportunity came sooner than she had expected, for the next week-end she went with her hostess to her Long Island home. As Mrs. Marriott had said it was indeed far more beautiful than the penthouse, a gracious ranch-home set in acres of beautiful countryside, and with a garden that sloped down to the shore.

"It's Long Island Sound," Mrs Marriott explained as she led Sara up to the bedroom. "In the Summer it's filled with yachts and if you do decide to stay on, you could learn sailing."

"Don't tempt me," Sara laughed, "or I might succumb."

"I wish you would," Mrs. Marriott said. "Now I've got some work to do, my dear, but I'll meet you downstairs for dinner."

Left alone Sara remained by the window looking out at the scene. Saturday afternoon at five o'clock. It was mid-day in England. Her mother would be shopping in the High Street, her father might be pottering around the garden and her young brother was no doubt playing with friends. A pang of homesickness overcame her and she put her head down on the window-sill and thought longingly of her parents. It was unthinkable to stay here more than three months! Afraid that if she did not do something active she would dissolve into tears, Sara unpacked her overnight case and then went exploring.

The house was vast. There were seven bedrooms, each with its own bathroom, and a huge games room which held a billiard table and also one for table tennis. On the ground floor there was an enormous living-room-cum-dining-room as well as a library which she did not enter, for she knew Mrs. Marriott was working there. But there were a great many other things to see; a kitchen twice the size of the one in the penthouse, a butler's pantry crammed full of silver, china and glass, and a breakfast-room gaily furnished with English chintz. Amazing the partiality Americans had for Scottish plaids and English chintz!

Outside she explored the grounds as best she could, unwilling to wander too far as dusk was already falling. She did however, come across the swimming pool and gazed at it in delight. It was unfilled at the moment since it was too cold to bathe, but even empty the azure blue tiles looked inviting and the diving boards seemed ready for the touch of a bare foot.

Opposite the swimming pool stood a row of cabanas and curiously she opened one and peeped inside. It was bare except for a shelf and a mirror and disappointed she drew back. She was just closing the door when she noticed something on the floor and she bent and picked it up. It was a picture of a girl, weather-beaten and faded, but recognisable as someone she knew. Sara frowned. Who could it be? She looked more closely at it, seeing the classical nose, the wide, curvaceous mouth and the almond shaped eyes. Almond shaped eyes! She blinked. No wonder she recognised the portrait. It bore a striking resemblance to herself! Trembling, Sara put the photograph in her pocket and went back to the house, convinced that at last she had managed to see what Sally Marriott looked like.

No-one could ever accuse Sara of being subtle. If she felt anything it was obvious in her face; if she believed in anything, what she believed was obvious in her actions. Tonight was no exception, for as she sat down at the table, she took the photograph out of her pocket and handed it across to her hostess. Mrs. Marriott turned white and the spoon in her hand clattered to the table.

"Where did you—where did you find it?"

"In one of the cabanas opposite the swimming pool."

"I see. I didn't know it was there. It's my daugher,

of course. You've guessed that." Sara nodded and Mrs.
Marriott made an effort to regain her composure. "I've
no other pictures of my daughter in the house. When
she left home I—I put them all away. The one you've
just found must have been lying there for quite some
time. She used those cabanas a great deal—she was
fond of swimming. I suppose she must have had some
pictures taken and stuffed one of them into the pocket
of her beach coat. It probably fell out."

"I'm glad it did. I was curious to see what she looked
like."

Mrs. Marriott stared at the photograph and, with
trembling hands turned it face down.

"Do you know where she is now?" Sara asked reck-
lessly, not caring whether the question was resented.

"No I don't. After Sally left I got in touch with a
detective agency and they told me she married her
boyfriend as soon as she left home. When I heard that,
I didn't bother with any more enquiries."

Sara digested this remark in silence. "If you had
your time over again, would you behave in the same
way?"

"I don't know. But it's pointless thinking about it.
I told you a little while ago that I couldn't afford the
luxury of having regrets. What is done cannot be un-
done."

"It's not true to say that," Sara said vehemently.
"As long as you're alive you can always try to alter
things."

"You say that because you're young," came the
reply. "When you're as old as I am you'll know that
some things can never be altered. Now I don't want to

talk about it anymore. That's an order, Sara."

Sara had no choice but to obey and for the rest of the meal they talked about other things. However when they left the table her quick eye noticed that the woman picked up the photograph and with a surreptitious movement slipped it into the bodice of her dress. No matter what Mrs. Marriott might say, she was not as immune to regrets as she believed.

CHAPTER X

IT was exhilarating to spend Spring in New York and Sara marvelled at how different it was from London. In England the change of seasons was much more obvious to the eye, for the moment the weather grew warmer, window-boxes sprouted into life and the parks which dappled the city glowed green. No matter whether one walked in Mayfair or traversed meaner streets in dingy suburbs, there was always a tree to be seen; an almond covered with blossom, a chestnut heavy with flowers. In New York however, this was not so, for apart from Central Park, there did not seem to be any greenery, and had it not been for her week-ends on Long Island Sara would sorely have missed the sight of leaves. Ever after, when she came to think of New York, she remembered it as a city of gleaming glass and concrete, of towering skyscrapers and roaring traffic; never of mellowness or greenness.

Yet Spring in New York was a notable affair and though there were few trees to sprout blossom and remind one that Summer was a-coming in, the shop windows did it instead!

Immediately after Christmas all the stores had ad-

vertised clothes for Winter cruises, but with the
coming of Spring they waxed even more enthusiastic
over the impending sunshine, and beach clothes were
displayed against mock sands, while parasols were
tilted invitingly over dummy bodies clad in pure silk
prints, ideal—so the posters said—for a leisurely day
in the mountains, an active day on the sea-shore or a
gay rendezvous in a restaurant in town.

There were so many things to do, so many different places to visit that Sara could well understand why
New Yorkers were so blasé. A few hours travel away
were the Catskill Mountains with their luxury hotels,
or if one preferred it one could go swimming in Long
Island Sound or walk the leafy lanes of New England,
more reminiscent of the "old world" than the New.

With the coming of Spring, Marriott's store had a
face-lift too. All the assistants changed out of their
dark dresses into grey and pink ones, and the same
grey and pink motif was seen in all the shopping bags
and wrapping paper covering every purchase made by
a customer. Mrs. Marriott was exceedingly busy, for
new items of merchandise were now appearing on the
counters and she would wander through each department four or five times a day to try and assess how the
new range of goods were selling. If they did not appear to be going fast enough to please her, she would
order it to be changed and when Sara commented
upon this on one occasion, Mrs. Marriott told her that
the price of everything in New York was so expensive
—and that included property—that her business
would run at a loss if they did not do an immediate
turnover.

"I can't bear to have things lying on the counters for days," she explained. "We must sell it at once."

The same rapid turnover had to take place in the ready-made dress department, and Sara had seen a complete rail of clothes disappear in less than an hour to be immediately replaced by another rail of entirely different design. Hard lines on any one who saw a dress advertised in a newspaper and came in later in the day to buy it!

The more Sara saw of the store the better pleased she was that she was not going to work in one permanently and she longed for the leisurely atmosphere of Donnell's where customers were treated as individuals and where it was not considered wrong to devote a whole hour to the discussion of a pleat or a drape!

Even when she was called on to model the Donnell Collection for a client she had to race against the clock and none of the customers deemed it necessary to look at a dress more than once before making up their minds whether or not to buy it. Although there was much to commend this American hustle, in some ways she found it less satisfying and longed for the day when a client would insist on seeing the same dress three or four times before making up her mind.

When Fate did decide to answer Sara's request, it did so in a way which made her regret she had ever wanted it to happen.

It was eleven o'clock on a Wednesday morning when Gina Banks rushed into the dressing-room where Sara was chatting to one of the assistants. She looked unusually flustered, and Sara realised why when she learnt that Grace Walderstein was asking to see the Donnell clothes. Ignorant though Sara was of New York society, even *she* had heard of this girl, heiress to ten million dollars, whose escapades had made the headlines regularly since her eighteenth birthday some three years ago.

"She wants to see suits and afternoon dresses," Gina said. "You'd better put on as many of the full-skirted ones as you can. Miss Walderstein likes that type best."

Excited at the thought of seeing this young woman, Sara hurriedly changed into a grey flannel suit piped with emerald green. As she modelled it she was aware of protruding brown eyes watching her and could not help a feeling of dislike as she noted the pale face with its wilful red mouth and insolent expression.

Grace Walderstein made no comment while Sara modelled the suits, but when she returned in the first dress—a bewitching affair of pink silk and organza—she gave an exclamation of pleasure and insisted that Sara twirl around the room to show the swing of the pleats.

"It's swell!" she said in a shrill voice. "I'll definitely have that one. But I'd like it made in black."

"Mr. Donnell only makes it in the colour that you see," Mrs. Banks said.

"Maybe he does," came the drawling reply, "but how does he happen to know the colour that suits *me?*"

"He doesn't. He merely knows the colour that suits the dress! And he was most explicit that pink is the only colour for this particular one. Mr. Donnell's an

exceptional man, that is why Mrs. Marriott was so delighted to procure his Collection."

"Well, at least he knows his own mind," Grace
Walderstein said as she hitched her mink stole around
her plump shoulders. "And that's more than can be
said for some of these guys! I guess he's right about
this colour. Though it must be tough on anyone who
wants it and doesn't happen to look good in pink."

It was fortuitous that the other dresses which the
American girl liked were available in a wide choice of
material, though Sara was amused when they were
chosen in the same colours as the original models.

"I rather go for this Donnell guy," the heiress said
finally. "He hasn't forgotten that he's designing for
women. Most of the Parisian and American designers
cater for beanpoles!"

Sara smiled at the remark and Grace Walderstein
frowned at her.

"What are *you* grinning about?"

"I'm sorry. I didn't realise it was noticeable."

"Well it was. And if it was a joke on me then I'd like
to share it."

"It wasn't a joke at all." Sara felt her cheeks redden.
"I was just—I was just pleased that you liked Mr.
Donnell's clothes."

"Oh were you? And what business is it of yours?"

Fearing an ugly scene, Gina Banks stepped forward. "Sara Gay is our new English model," she explained. "Mrs. Marriott brought her over from
London."

"How come? Aren't the models here good enough?"

"Sara works for Donnell's."

When she heard this the American turned and looked at her, a speculative glance that made Sara feel as if she were in a cattle market being auctioned for sale.

"So you work for this guy Donnell? Come over here and tell me about him. How old is he and what does he look like?"

Reluctant though she was to discuss Marc, Sara had no choice and gave the answers as briefly as possible.

"Gee, you're making him sound a real humdinger. I'm going to Europe in a few weeks time and I'll step off and see him. In fact, I don't think I'll have any of these clothes after all. I'll get him to design new ones for me. Then I'll be sure that no-one else will be wearing the same styles!"

Gina's mouth dropped open in dismay, but remembering that the customer was always right, she forced a smile to her face.

"It's a pity you've changed your mind. I'm sure Mr. Donnell will be delighted to design some clothes especially for you, but he would have been flattered if you'd arrived wearing one of his things, particularly if you'd bought it here. He's most anxious to break into the American market, and you're such a trend-setter . . . . So many girls will follow you once you put your stamp of approval on something . . ."

The woman continued to enthuse and Sara was amused to see Grace Walderstein lap up every word, finally agreeing to take the clothes after all.

Sara was on her way back to the dressing room when Grace Walderstein called her back. "Bring that pink dress out again, will you? I want to see it."

"Do you want me to model it for you?"

"Yes. And hurry up. I haven't got all day."

Sara bit back an angry retort and hurried out. She had modelled for some spoiled and rude women in her time, but never for one quite as ungracious. With trembling fingers she put on the pink dress and made her entrance again.

"Yeah," the heiress drawled. "It looks even better when you see it a second time. The only thing is, does pink suit me?"

"It's exactly your colour," Gina commented. "It's ideal with your dark hair and eyes."

"I don't need you to make up my mind for me," came the rude reply.

"I'm sorry. I thought you were asking me a question."

"I wasn't asking anybody a question. I just happened to be talking out loud."

Grace Walderstein stood up and came over to Sara, pushing her unceremoniously over to a mirror. "I wonder if I should try it on myself? I'm just about your figure."

"I think I'm a little thinner," Sara murmured.

"Well, I'm not a skeleton like you that's for sure. But I can still get into that dress and look a darn sight better in it than you do."

Before Sara realised what was happening, she felt hard fingers pressing into her back and heard the wrench of the zip.

"Be careful!" Sara gasped. "It's flimsy fabric."

She spoke too late. There was a rending sound and as the dress fell to the floor she saw that the whole of one side of it had been ripped away from the zip, and ripped so uncompromisingly that there was no hope of repairing it without it being visible.

"Now look what you've done," Grace Walderstein screamed. "Why did you have to twist around while I was undoing it?"

"I didn't twist round," Sara declared hotly. "You pulled it so roughly that—"

"Are you trying to tell me I don't know how to undo a dress? I've never had anybody speak to me like that before. Mrs. Banks!" she screamed. "Come here at once!"

Gina came running over. While Sara and her client had been standing in front of the mirror, she had taken the opportunity to talk to another customer who had been waiting patiently during the whole session. Now, in one glance, she realised what had happened and her face paled.

"This model of yours is trying to blame me for ruining the dress. It was her fault entirely. She turned round as I was undoing the zip and she gave a jerk that—"

"I did nothing of the sort," Sara protested.

"Yes you did! And you did it purposely because you didn't like me saying you had a lousy figure."

"Why you rotten little liar!" Sara lost her temper and her eyes sparkled green. "How dare you talk to me like that? You might be rich in money, Miss Walderstein, but you're very poor in manners!"

"Hear hear," said a soft voice with a southern accent, and they turned and stared in surprise at a rotund woman wrapped in mink who had come over to them.

"The model is telling the truth," she said. "I was watching the whole thing. Miss Walderstein tore the dress. She always was a clumsy child, even when she was at school!"

Had the situation not been so serious, Sara could almost have laughed at the look of incredulity on Grace's face. It grew as red as a turkeycock and the pale eyes bulged alarmingly.

"Who do you think you are?" she spluttered. "How do you know what I was like at school?"

"I'm Amy Sutherland," the plump woman said quietly. "Mary Sutherland is my granddaughter and you both were at school in Vermont. Even now she speaks of her schooldays with you as being the un-happiest ones of her life. But I really think you're old enough now to learn how to behave." She turned back to Gina. "Your model is entirely blameless. If you have to debit anyone with the cost of this dress, you should debit it to Grace."

"I'm not going to pay for any dress," Grace shouted furiously. "And I'll thank you to mind your own business!"

"Please, please," Gina said quickly. "Everybody's looking."

By now a crowd had gathered round, murmuring and nudging one another as they recognised the American heiress. Quick to sense the interest of an audience, Grace Walderstein drew herself up to her full height.

"I don't intend to stay here and be insulted. Either

you dismiss this girl immediately or I'll never set foot in the store again."

"Please," Gina pleaded. "I'd like to help you, you're an important client—but I can't dismiss Miss Gay. The only person who can do that is Mrs. Marriott."

"Then you'd better send for her at once!"

"That won't be necessary," said a firm voice. "I'm here already!"

CHAPTER XI

PETITE and dainty though she was, Tina Marriott exuded a force and magnetism which could not be denied and even Grace Walderstein, cocooned in the security of wealth, felt this presence and lost some of her bombastic attitude.

"Thank goodness you're here," she said in sulky tones. "I've had about as much as I intend taking from your staff. I want you to fire this model right away."

"On what grounds?"

"Insolence. She ruined a Donnell dress I'd set my heart on. She couldn't bear the thought of my trying it on and she deliberately tore it."

Mrs. Marriott looked at Sara. "Is that true?"

Before Sara could reply the American girl intervened. "Aren't you going to take *my* word for it? Do you have to ask *her* what happened?"

"I like to hear both sides of the story, Miss Walderstein. I saw part of what happened as I was walking through the department, but I wish to hear the rest of it. Now then, Sara . . . ."

Fighting back the tears, Sara told her employer what had taken place.

"It was an accident," she finished. "As I turned round the material ripped and—"

"I can hardly believe you would turn round so violently that the material would rip. It must have been pulled extremely roughly." Mrs. Marriott fingered the ruined dress between her hands. "No Sara, I appreciate you're trying to be helpful, but there's no reason for you to take the blame. It's entirely Miss Walderstein's fault."

"How dare you say that!" the heiress screeched. "I spend a fortune in this place and if you don't fire this girl at once I'll never set foot in here again. And I'll see my friends don't either!"

"Much as we would be sorry to lose your custom," the answer came back instantly, "I have no intention of altering the policy of my store, which is fairness at all costs. Sometimes the fairness applies to the customer and sometimes—on occasions like this—it protects the employee. You ruined the dress by your own bad temper, Miss Walderstein and the bill will be sent to you."

"My lawyers will deal with this."

"No doubt they will. And mine will do likewise." Mrs. Marriott dumped the dress into Gina Banks' arms. "Wrap it up and send it to Miss Walderstein. The quicker the whole thing's forgotten the better."

Majestically she made her way through the crowd and Grace Walderstein stared after her venomously.

"I've never been so insulted in my life," she hissed. "I'll see this story gets into the papers. I'll sue her . . . I'll . . ."

Not waiting to hear any more, Sara fled. In the

dressing-room she hurriedly put on another dress and repaired make-up which tears had ravaged. What a horrible experience it had been.

"Don't look so upset, child," Gina Banks said behind her. "She always was a most unpleasant girl. It'll be a pleasure not having to serve her any more."

"But won't she be a big loss? I mean she must spend an awful lot of money here."

"So do lots of other women. Anyway, there was nothing else Mrs. Marriott could have done except handle it the way she did. She was superb, wasn't she? But whenever she's faced with something like this she's always icy calm."

Unexpectedly Sara wondered whether her employer had been icy calm with her own daughter. How disastrous such behaviour would have been.

"You're looking pretty shaken, Sara," Gina said suddenly. "Why not put on your coat and go for a stroll? There's no-one down in the Appointment Book for the rest of the day."

"I wouldn't mind a breath of fresh air," Sara confessed and reached for her coat and scarf.

She was on the point of entering the elevator when she changed her mind and decided she could not go out until she had seen Mrs. Marriott and apologised for what had happened. Maybe there was something she could do to put things right. A letter of apology —much as she hated the thought—to Grace Walderstein, perhaps?

She made her way to the top floor where the Accounts Department and executive offices were housed. Mrs. Marriott's suite was at the far end and as

Sara entered it she found herself confronted by a battery of secretaries. Luckily one of them recognised her and, as if Mrs. Marriott had been expecting her and had left orders for her to be seen immediately, Sara was ushered into the inner sanctum.

Half expecting the same splendour as the penthouse she was surprised to find the room austere, almost masculine in its concept though the severity was softened by numerous bowls of spring flowers.

Behind a massive eight foot desk arrayed with telephones, sat the owner of this vast empire, the light which streamed in from the window behind her turning her hair into a silver halo.

"I was expecting you," she said, thus confirming the girl's earlier suspicions. "I suppose you've come to talk about Grace."

"Yes. I feel so guilty about it. She didn't like me. I felt that from the beginning and when she made that remark about my figure, well . . . . I shouldn't have told her I was thinner than she was. That made her madder than ever!"

"There was still no need for her to destroy the dress. I'm sure she did it deliberately in a fit of temper. No, Sara, the incident is closed. I said that downstairs and I meant it."

"But she's such a good customer . . . If I wrote to her and apologised . . ."

"The incident is closed, I tell you. If I—"

One of the telephones rang and Mrs. Marriott picked it up. Although she did not wish to listen Sara couldn't help overhearing the conversation, which she gathered was with a prominent New York interior decorator called D'Arcy. But prominent though he was, it was obvious Mrs Marriott had found him unsatisfactory and Sara could not help smiling at the woman's cutting references to the schemes he had submitted for her new building on Long Island.

"I know I said I wanted something feminine, but the designs you've submitted are more suitable for the Palace at Versailles . . . No, I *don't* like golden chandeliers in the Dress Department. Nor did I like the silver-gilt counters!"

There was more conversation in a similar vein and when at last the call came to an end Sara was grinning openly.

"You certainly told him a thing or two."

"Much good it'll do me," her employer said drily. "I'm in a pretty fix now. I was relying on D'Arcy's schemes but they're simply dreadful. Interior decorators seem to be in two camps. Either theatrical ones who only work well for the stage, or else purely functional ones who only design for offices." She spread her hands wide. "My new store will cater for suburbanites and most of them will be women. I want an atmosphere of leisure and discreet luxury. But too much luxury will make them think they're being taken for a ride pricewise."

"But your things *are* expensive."

"Not when you really look at them. We give value for money at Marriott's. The customer won't think so though if all she can see in the departments are gold chandeliers and thickly carpeted floors! No, Sara, I know exactly the way I want the decor done but I can't put it into words." She tapped her forehead. "It's

all here and if I could see it on paper I'd know immediately if it were right. There's one other young man I
could try."

As she spoke she picked up a telephone pad and
turned the pages. "Now what's his number? Darn, I
can't see a thing without my glasses. Here, Sara, tell
me the number would you? The name is Hart. Montgomery Hart."

Taking the pad, Sara looked down the H's: Harri-
son, Harwich, Harvey, Harcourt Detective Agency,
Hart. Ah, there it was. Montgomery Hart, Murray
Hill 23541. She spoke the number aloud and Mrs.
Marriott dialled it.

Sara only half listened to the conversation for as she
put the telephone pad back on the desk a shiver of
excitement ran through her. On this pad were all the
private numbers Mrs. Marriott used; her friends, her
acquaintances, her tradespeople and even her detective agency! There was no doubt this was the very
detective agency she had used to find out what had
happened to her daughter after she had run away.
Surely they would still know where the girl was, or if
not, still have her last known address?

Although aware that she was interfering in something that was no concern of hers, she felt Fate had
brought her to this office today. Fate had put the telephone pad in her hands and the name of the detective
agency in front of her eyes. Firmly she memorised
the name, repeating it over and over in her mind.

"Sara, I'm speaking to you." With a start she realised Mrs. Marriott was standing by her side. "I have
to see someone now, but I'll be home early tonight."

"Of course. I'm sorry to have kept you so long."

"Don't be sorry. I'm always delighted to talk to you —even in business hours!"

Once in the store, Sara decided she would still accept Gina's offer to go for a stroll and she went down into the street. People jostled her on either side but so immersed in her thoughts was she that she did not notice how far she had walked until a policeman put his hand on her arm as she was stepping off the kerb.

"The lights are against you," he warned. "You cross when they're green and I'll give you a ticket!"

Sara murmured an apology and the policeman's frown disappeared.

"You're a Limey, aren't you? I was in London during the war."

He spoke to Sara at some length of his sojourn there and then ended up by cautioning her again about crossing against the lights.

"It's no offence to do so in England," he remarked, "but it should be."

"Oh yes, it should," agreed Sara and escaped from his benign eye.

She had indeed walked much further than she intended, and had reached one of the busiest sectors of New York: Forty-Second Street. On one side of her lay Macy's and on the other Gimbles, two of the largest mass-market stores, and certainly the places where she would obtain all her presents before returning home! Mrs. Marriott might talk about her own store giving value for money, but one needed more money than Sara possessed in order to shop there.

"Forty-Second Street," she mused as she walked down it. Hadn't there been a song of that name in her mother's time and a musical picture? But for the moment it was neither the song nor the musical that held her interest, but the knowledge that in this vicinity was the Harcourt Detective Agency.

Unfortunately she did not know the exact address and she looked for a telephone kiosk. She could not remember ever having seen one and she made her way to the nearest Underground station. How silly she had felt the first time she had asked someone where the Underground was and they had looked at her and said: "Are you telling me to drop dead?"

When she had explained she merely wanted an underground train they had laughed and advised her to use the word "subway". Now she hurried to the Forty-Second Street subway and reached a small telephone cubicle complete with battered directory. Quickly she looked up the address she wanted and, returning to the daylight, set off at a brisk pace towards the West Side.

What a good thing it was that all addresses were numbers instead of names for she could easily work out how long it would take her to arrive at her destination. Five blocks to the left and two to the right. Deciding that unless she hurried she would be away from the store most of the afternoon she signalled a taxi.

Within minutes she was deposited outside a plate-glass skyscraper and whisked up in one of the elevators to the twenty-eighth floor. Every room held the office of a different firm, the majority of them being theatrical agencies and music publishers. The one at the far end was the one she was looking for and she knocked on the door and went in.

A young man at a desk looked at her with obvious admiration as she nervously asked to see Mr. Harcourt.

"Can you tell me what it's about?"

"It's about . . . about a Miss Marriott."

Curiosity was written on his face but as if realising he would get nothing further from her he disappeared into an inner room and emerged almost at once to usher her inside. He closed the door and Sara found herself alone with a middle-aged man resembling her father.

"I'm Dave Harcourt," he said extending his hand. "And you are?"

"Sara Gay. I work for Mrs. Marriott."

"I see. And she sent you to me?"

"No. As a matter of fact I—"

Wondering how to begin Sara hesitated and then decided it would facilitate matters just to plainly state what she wanted.

"I'm trying to get in touch with Sally Marriott, and I don't want to ask her mother for her last address."

"It wouldn't help if you did. The one we have is more than a year old and I doubt if she's still there. I can give it to you though, if it'll be of any help. But you understand Mrs. Marriott stopped us from making any further enquiries once we found out her daughter was married." He rummaged in his drawer and brought out a tattered folder. He wrote something down on a pad and then tore out the slip of paper and handed it to her. "Here it is for what it's worth."

She put the paper in her handbag. "I'm very grateful to you, Mr. Harcourt. Thanks awfully."

"Do you want it for any special reason?"

"No, just . . . . It's just that I'm hoping to try and patch things up between them."

"You must be an optimist. That Mrs. Marriott's a tough cookie."

Sara said nothing and moved to the door.

"Hey there," he called. "If you do decide to go to that address take a tip from me, will you?"

"Yes?"

"Don't go there at night. It's a tricky sort of neighbourhood."

Chastened Sara left the office and returned to the street.

CHAPTER XII

SARA was anxious to visit Sally Marriott's last address at once, but she had already been away too long from the store and reluctantly she returned there.

Even in the evening she was unable to go on her errand for Mr. Harcourt's last words rang menacingly in her ears, and though the slip of paper sent out exciting signals to her, she ignored them as best she could and sat in the sumptious living-room writing a letter home and uncomfortably aware of Mrs. Marriott sitting opposite her, reading.

"I'm surprised you don't go out on any dates," the woman said unexpectedly. "I'd have thought a pretty girl like you would be inundated with them. At that party I took you to last week I saw at least three of the young men ask for your phone number."

"I didn't give it to them," Sara said. "I find most boys of my own age too young, and if they're older then they've got different ideas—generally the wrong ideas as far as I'm concerned!"

"I don't think it's the age you object to, my dear. After all, Marc Donnell is older than you."

Sara blushed furiously. "But we've lots of things in common. I'm never bored with him and—"

"You've certainly got lots of things in common. He thinks he's got a great talent and you think so too! In fact, you could form an admiration society for Marc Donnell."

Surprised at what she considered such an unwarranted attack on the designer, Sara hotly denied this.

"Marc's the least conceited man I know. Why before every Collection he practically has a fit in case it'll be a flop. And you wouldn't grudge him being conceited if you knew how hard he works."

"Hey there, I'm not criticising your young man. I'm merely trying to point out that he's not perfect and that you should give yourself a chance to go out with other boys instead of holding a candle for just one."

"I'm not holding a candle for Marc. You're just as bad as Betsy and Beryl—they're two friends of mine who are always saying the same thing."

"Probably because it's true! Anyway it isn't right for you not to go out with other boys. The greater your experience the better it'll be for you when you make your final choice."

"I won't make a final choice for at least another ten years," Sara said vehemently. "I want to get to the top in my profession, and I can't do that if I'm married and have a home and children to look after."

Mrs. Marriott seemed amused at this, but said nothing further, though she could not hold back a pleasurable exclamation when the telephone rang some half hour later and Sara, after taking it, returned to say it was one of the young men whom she had met at last week's party.

"Heaven knows how he got my number. *I* didn't

tell him I was staying with you. Anyway, he's taking me out to dinner." She grinned and flung her arms round Mrs. Marriott's neck. "You're right, you know —it's silly of me to sit at home all the time. I mean, if I do I'll just end up an old stick in the mud, won't I?"

Truth to tell, Sara had another reason for accepting Bobby Walker's invitation. She could not try and find Sally Marriott during the day and she could not go alone in the evening. But with a husky American male by her side . . . . Giggling at her duplicity, Sara undressed that night and climbed between the sheets, wondering what the wealthy young Mr. Walker would say when he collected her tomorrow and she told him that instead of going to a swanky night spot she wanted to go to a sleazy downtown apartment house!

Sara had misjudged the resilience of her escort, for though he had obviously intended taking her to a smart restaurant, he made no objection when—the moment they were in his car—she asked him if he would mind driving her to the other side of New York.

"Anything you say, baby," he said agreeably. "Though when a guy takes a girl on a date over here *he's* generally the one to name the place! Still, if you know a nice joint downtown . . ."

"I don't know any "joint" downtown," she said vehemently. "I want to call on a friend of mine."

"Living there?" he asked incredulously. "Whoever it is they must be down on their luck. It's almost Skid Row where the drunks hang out."

Sara's heart sank at the thought of a girl used to living in a penthouse now living near Skid Row. She glanced at the boy behind the wheel of the car and decided to tell him the truth. There was something likeable about this rangy young man with the freckled face and blond crew cut.

"As a matter of fact, I'm trying to find Sally Marriott and this place is the last address I have of hers."

"Gee! Aren't you meddling with something that doesn't concern you?"

"It's got to concern somebody," Sara said sharply. "Mrs. Marriott's very unhappy and I think Sally should be made to realise it."

"The old girl doesn't look unhappy to me."

"Well, she is."

Sara did not mention the times when she had heard sobs coming from Mrs. Marriott's bedroom nor the moments when the smile had left the autocratic face to be replaced by a look of loneliness and sadness. These were intimacies not to be shared, but merely stored in one's own mind and acted upon—as she was acting upon them now.

As they drove further downtown the streets became dingier and the buildings more squalid and the smells more rancid. At last they drew up outside a rooming house with flaking paint and filthy windows.

"This is it," Bobby said. "Want to go up on your own?"

"Wouldn't you like to come with me?" Sara said brightly.

"Not much." Then as her face fell, he grinned. "I was only teasing. I've no intention of letting you go in there alone."

They entered the building and looked expectantly

at a shirt-sleeved man yawning his way towards them.

"We're full up," he grunted.

"We don't want a room," Sara said quickly. "We're looking for—" She stopped, horrified, for she did not know Sally's married name. That was one thing she had forgotten to ask Mr. Harcourt.

The proprietor looked at her suspiciously. "Who did you say you're looking for?"

"A girl called Sally," Bobby put in belligerently. "She lived here a while back."

The man yawned again and looked at Sara. "Your sister, huh? I'd have known it anywhere." He scratched his head. "She's not here now. Left about six months ago. I don't know where she moved but maybe my wife does. Hey, Maria!"

A black-haired woman came out from a room behind the stairs, her shapeless body enclosed in a print dress.

"Maria, do you know where Mrs. Lambert moved to when she left here?"

The woman nodded, her gold ear-rings gleaming. "Ten blocks away," she volunteered and smiled at Sara "Same place like this, but no stairs so it was easier for her. She was having a bad time and couldn't walk much. That's why her husband found the other place."

Sara was perturbed by what she had just learned. "Was Sally ill?"

"Not ill. But having a difficult time." Maria sighed and smiled shyly. "There is no need to worry anymore. It'll be over by now."

Sara's anxiety grew. What would be over by now?

Had she come too late? Was Sally dead?

As if knowing what was going through her mind, Bobby asked the next question. "How can you be so sure it's over?"

The woman chuckled, her fat body shaking with laughter. "I mightn't have gone to school, Mister, but I can add! Babies take nine months to come and Sally Lambert must have been a mother for the last three months!"

Outside in the street Sara and Bobby stared at one another.

"Well," he said pushing her into the car. "Now we've managed to get the new address I suppose you want to follow it through?"

"How did you guess?"

"Masculine intuition! Here was I looking forward to a swell evening showing off the prettiest girl in the town and what am I doing? Driving from one dump to another trying to find a girl who'll probably give you the bird when you *do* locate her!"

"Did you know Sally?" Sara asked curiously, ignoring his earlier remarks.

"Not very well. I was at University when she left home, but I heard from my mother of the shennanigans that went on." He peered through the window and flashed on his headlights. "We're here now," he grunted. "Let's hope we have better luck."

Almost before the car came to a stop Sara had jumped out and run up the steps of the boarding house. The door was closed and she rang the bell. There was no reply and she rang again. Footsteps echoed on the bare boards and as the door creaked open a truculent voice asked them what they wanted. Sara drew back nervously, relieved to bump against Bobby.

"We want to see Mrs. Lambert," she said firmly.

The door creaked open wider and in the dim light she saw an old man in the faded remnants of a commissionaire's suit.

"Ground floor back," he said. "You'll hear the kid crying."

With some trepidation Sara and Bobby walked down the hall to the last door. Contrary to what the old man had said there was no sound of a baby crying. In fact, there was no sound at all and with trembling hands she knocked.

Hardly had her hand dropped to her side when the door was opened by a young man of Bobby's height, in grey flannels and a tartan shirt. He was one of the handsomest men Sara had ever seen with dark skin, black hair and glittering dark eyes that reminded her of Marc.

"Are you Mr. Lambert?" she asked quickly.

"Yes. Who are you?"

"You won't know me. My name is Sara Gay and I'm looking for Sally Marriott—I mean Sally Lambert."

"Well, come on in."

He beckoned them to enter and they stepped into a large, bed-sitting room. There was no-one else in it and Sara looked round in disappointment. "Isn't your wife here?"

For answer he raised his voice and at the call of her name a tall, slim girl carrying a white bundle came in from what was obviously the kitchen.

"What is it, Garry?" she began and stopped as she saw the visitors. Her face changed colour as she recognised Bobby Walker. "What are you doing here?" she asked sharply.

"I don't know. Better ask the girl who brought me."

Sara stepped forward. Too late now to wonder whether she had done the right thing. She was here and would have to make the best of it.

"I work at Marriott's," she said, "and I'm living with your mother. She misses you."

"Did she send you to say so?"

"She doesn't know I'm here."

The two girls looked at one another, and Sara found it astonishing to see an older edition of herself. Not that they were really alike when judged together, for Sally Marriott was thinner, with a darker skin and hair verging on auburn rather than red-gold. But there was certainly enough of a likeness for them to be mistaken for sisters. It was a likeness Sally noticed too, but a scornful smile curved the corners of her mouth.

"What's mother done?" she queried. "Adopted you as a daughter?"

"I told you I work for her. I'm a model and I'm staying at the store for three months."

"Oh, I remember now. I read something about it in the papers." The girl clutched the bundle more closely in her arms. "But I don't know why you're here. If Mother had wanted to find me she could have done so easily enough."

"Maybe she was waiting for *you* to find her!"

"I'll never go back! Not after the things she said

about Garry. I've made my way of life and I don't want any other."

Her husband stepped forward and placed his arm around her shoulder. "Don't get upset about it, Sal. This young lady's only trying to help."

Sara smiled at him gratefully. "Mrs. Marriott has no idea I'm here. She'd be furious if she found out."

Sally shrugged. "You're wasting your time. Mother and I have nothing to say to one another any more. And I'm not going to let anyone tell me how to run my life."

"But she's your mother. Don't you love her?"

The girl seemed taken aback by the question and turning away she placed the bundle in a carry-cot that stood on a divan in the corner.

"Of course I love her," she said tonelessly. "Though it wasn't easy to love someone who was hardly ever there! She only found time for me when I was intelligent enough to talk to her and interesting enough for her to take around. As a kid she couldn't be bothered with me."

Sara felt the precious moments slipping away and with each one that passed, hope of a reconciliation faded. Desperately she said the first thing that came into her head.

"Your baby—is it a boy or girl?"

"A girl. She's three months old today."

Sara stepped forward and Sally moved the blanket down for her to see the rosy face with its cupid's bow mouth and soft cheeks.

"What a beauty," Sara murmured. "You must have fun with her."

"Not enough fun. Garry and I leave her with a foster mother during the day so that we can go out to work."

Sara remained looking at the sleeping child.

"I hope you won't have to go on working for long. If you do your baby might grow up to say exactly the same things about *you* that you're saying about your mother."

"I'm working to give my child a decent way of life! I'm not concerned with giving it luxuries. Just bread and jam."

"Your mother wasn't concerned to give you luxuries in the beginning either. Or do you only think of her now as being rich? Maybe you've forgotten that when you were a child she was as poor as you are now."

Sally turned away, the graceful line of her neck infinitely pathetic. Garry moved close to his wife and put his arms around her.

"The young lady's got a point," he said huskily. "Maybe you should make it up with your mother again."

"No! I can't forget the things she said about you. Going to see her won't help us any. She said you were a fortune hunter, a penniless—"

"Beatnik," Sara concluded. "I gathered everybody thought he was a beatnik!"

The young couple looked at her and Garry suddenly started to laugh. "I suppose I was when I was at Art School and first met Sal. But it's a phase most arty people go through, and I've grown out of it now." He grunted. "There's nothing like marriage and a baby for knocking the beatnik out of one!"

A cry came from the corner of the room and they looked towards the carry-cot where a flailing arm could be seen beating the air. Sally hurried over and rocked the cot gently until the cries had subsided.

Sara tip-toed forward to look at the baby again. It was awake now and stared at her with large, blue eyes. Slowly it's mouth opened and it gave a gummy grin. Even without teeth and dribbling slightly it bore a weird resemblance to its maternal grandmother!

"Mrs. Marriott would love you," Sara murmured and Sally drew a sharp breath and stepped back from the cot.

"When I see my Mother again—if ever I do—" she said fiercely, "it'll be when Garry's proved himself and we can go back and tell her how wrong she was to judge him the way she did."

Sara found it difficult to argue against this reasoning, for had she been in a similar position she would have done exactly the same thing.

It was a decision however which appeared to make Garry uneasy, for he frowned. "Don't have any false pride on my account, honey. I've told you that before."

Sally rubbed her hand against his shoulder but remained looking at Sara. "We had a difficult time to begin with, but things are much better now. Once Garry finished his studies he got a job immediately."

"I'm sure he did." Bobby entered the conversation, his open face expressing his embarrassment at the situation in which he found himself. "There's no need to get so het up about it. Your mother might have had reservations about your husband, but Sara and I haven't. That's why we came to find you. I'm sure that now Garry's qualified as an art teacher he'll be able to—"

"Hey, let's get this straight," Garry spoke nervously, colour staining his cheeks. "I might have qualified as an art teacher, but I'm not practising as one. Sure I've got a job, but Sal didn't tell you what it was. I'm a lift boy at Macy's."

"Garry!" his wife cried.

"That's all right, Sal. These two have got to know the truth." He looked from Sara to Bobby. "I want to be an interior decorator but I want to work my way and no-one else's. That makes it pretty difficult to get a job with a firm. When they buy your services they don't want to buy your talent! So rather than turn out stuff which I'd be ashamed of, I prefer to work an elevator."

"You've sure got some pride," Bobby grinned. "Personally I'd say that if you worked for someone and followed their ideas for a while then they'd be prepared to listen to some of your schemes."

"That's the quickest way to get bogged down," Garry said. "I've seen it happen to my friends. Lots of them took steady jobs and hoped that eventually the boss would let them do things their way. But it's never worked out like that. You should see the rubbish they're turning out. Madame Pompadour apartments for rich matrons or stuff that's so modern that nobody can live with it."

Sara shook her head slightly. These were words she had heard from Mrs. Marriott, and one wondered what Garry would say were she to tell him that his

mother-in-law agreed with his views entirely and because of it was having trouble in finding decorators
for her new store!

Diplomatically she decided to say nothing, and
turned instead to Sally.

"Well, even if you won't meet your mother, I still
hope you'll let *me* come and see you sometimes?"

"Oh sure, come any time you want." Sally smiled
for the first time and it made a world of difference to
her face, giving her back her youth and making Sara
realise that the girl was only a few years her senior.
"Though why you want to come all the way out here
I can't imagine."

"It's simple. After all, it isn't every day of the week
that one meets one's double!"

Sally laughed. "I know what you mean. I got quite
a shock when I saw you." She pushed back her hair
from her forehead. "Come over by all means. I'd like
to know more about England and with that accent of
yours I could hear you talk all day!"

"Would it be all right if I came over one evening? I
work during the day and at week-ends I—I go out to
Long Island."

"Mother's little protegée, eh?" The words were bitter and realising they might sound jealous, Sally
apologised for them. "I didn't mean that. Forgive
me."

"That's all right," Sara said, and decided to strike
while the iron was hot. "How about next Tuesday?"

"Fine. Come for supper. I'm not the world's best
cook, but I'm sure better than I was when I first got
married."

"You couldn't be worse," Garry said wryly. "Have you ever known anyone ruin baked beans?"

Laughing at this remark, Sara and Bobby moved to the door. Sally came with them as far as the hall and as Sara was turning to go outside she caught her arm.

"If you come here it's only on the understanding that you don't tell my Mother where I am. I meant it when I said I didn't want to see her."

"Very well. I won't say a word."

Driving along Fifth Avenue, Sara thought about Sally and her husband and the fat and happy-looking baby in its carry-cot. What would Mrs. Marriott say when she discovered she was a grandmother? It was an answer Sara knew she would not be able to find out for a long time, for she realised that Sally would need a lot of persuading before she could forget the quarrel she had had with her mother. Obstinate Mrs. Marriott certainly was, but it was nothing compared with the obstinacy of her daughter!

CHAPTER XIII

SARA could not help feeling sorry for the way she had treated Bobby Walker who, expecting to take her out to a smart restaurant and show her off to his friends, had found himself escorting her from one tenement to another. He had behaved so well over the whole thing that she agreed to go out with him the following night, and he arranged to call for her at the same time.

Mrs. Marriott was surprised when she learned Sara was going out with Bobby Walker two nights in succession, and since Sara could not explain the reason, she had to suffer some teasing from her hostess, who assumed that love had bloomed!

"I knew you'd like him," she said with a complacent little smile, "and his parents are charming too. His father's a doctor and specialises in weight reduction."

"He must earn a fortune then!" Sara grinned. "I've never known women so diet conscious as they are over here."

"We're *youth* conscious, that's the real reason. Every woman over forty is determined to look like her daughter for as long as possible."

"I don't know why. My mother's never tried to make herself look younger than she is and she's perfectly happy. My father would throw a fit if she dyed her hair or tried to lose weight."

"Your mother's a lucky woman then. In this country, husband's like their wives to look like glamour girls."

"Oh men," Sara said in scathing tones. "They never know what they like! If one of them fell in love with me he'd have to take me as I was—all the time!"

"Luckily you're a natural born glamour girl," Mrs. Marriott laughed, "so you've nothing to worry about!"

"So are you," Sara said. "I mean you're the one person I know who manages to look your age and be beautiful at the same time."

"What a lovely compliment, Sara. Not very diplomatically put, but nonetheless appreciated." She touched her silver hair. "This isn't real you know."

Sara gaped at her in astonishment. "Do you mean it's dyed?"

"Of course. My hair used to be auburn like—" she hesitated, "like Sally's. Then it began to turn grey and look like pepper and salt. Nothing's more ageing than that kind of hair, and I was faced with the choice of either dyeing it auburn again or going silver. I decided on silver since I knew I could never get it the auburn shade it had once been."

"How typical of you," Sara giggled. "You're the woman with no regrets, and you were determined not to regret your auburn hair either."

"Exactly! Anyway, silver's much more flattering to a fading skin."

"Sally's hair is a beautiful shade."

Mrs. Marriott's breakfast cup clattered on to the saucer. "How do you know? Have you seen her?"

Sara swallowed hard. "That picture—the one I found in the cabana—it was coloured."

"I see." Mrs. Marriott pushed back her chair as if she had not only lost her appetite for food but also for continuing the conversation. "I must leave for the office or I'll be late," she said abruptly. "As you're going out with Bobby tonight I'll dine with friends."

That evening Sara left the store as early as she could and hurried back to the penthouse to change. She owed it to Bobby to look her best and she debated which dress to wear as she rode up in the elevator: a tight-fitting dinner dress in lemon coloured wild silk, or a full-skirted one in shades of mauve, lilac and pink, an unusual combination with her red-gold hair, but one which was so striking that it always brought her compliments. When she entered her bedroom, however, all thoughts of either disappeared from her mind, for on the bed reposed a letter with an English postmark and picking it up she recognised the heavy bold handwriting: Marc Donnell.

It was the first letter she had received from him and she opened it quickly, her annoyance that she had not heard from him before, disappearing as she read the closely written pages. They gave her a brief account of what had happened at the salon since she had left it, told her of the new customers that had come and one or two older ones who had gone.

"I've engaged a temporary model to take your place, one of those who helped out at our last Collection, and though she's a nice girl she can't compare with you. At the risk of making you conceited—very little risk, I know, because you're the least conceited girl I've met—I must tell you I miss you and long for your return. Believe me, Sara, it will be a long time before I'll allow anyone else to borrow your services.

"I'm sorry I haven't written before, but I find it difficult to express what I have to in words. It's much easier for me to say what I wish with material, so if you look in your wardrobe you might begin to appreciate how much I'm missing you. If you wonder how things have been arranged so fortuitously ask Mrs. Marriott since she was in on the secret."

The letter dropped to the bed and Sara rushed across to the wardrobe. All the dresses she had brought with her from England were hanging there, but she saw none of them, her eye caught instead by a glittering creation of white chiffon spangled with silver beads and pearls.

Reverently she took it down and held it against her. This was what Marc meant when he said he could express himself more easily in fabric! Somehow she was afraid to analyse exactly what he wanted this dress to mean, for it betokened an emotion that she feared might sweep her off her feet—and those feet had many rungs of the ladder to climb before they would willingly allow themselves to be swept off the ground!

Quickly she bathed and made up and then slipped the dress over her shoulders. There seemed hundreds of tiny hooks and eyes to fasten but at last they were all completed and, stepping into a pair of transparent plastic shoes with high jewelled heels, she looked at herself in the glass. A fairy-tale princess stared back at her; creamy shoulders rising from a spangled bodice and tiny waist gripped by draped chiffon that billowed out in gossamer clouds around her shapely legs.

"Just wait till Bobby sees this," she gloated. "It'll knock him in the eye!"

Knock him in the eye it certainly did, for Bobby's face was a study when Sara came to the door at his ring.

"Oh boy," he said, "oh boy! Just wait till my friends get a load of you!"

Proud as a turkey cock he escorted her some little while later into a gaily lit restaurant packed with tables. The noise was deafening and a three piece orchestra in the corner added its own clamour to the general confusion. But the food was superlatively good, thick steaks being a speciality. Chico's was the favourite rendezvous of most of Bobby's contemporaries and during the entire meal other young men came to the table to be introduced to Sara.

Soon Bobby began to tire of the constant interruptions and when dinner was over he hurried Sara away.

"I'm not taking you to that place again in a hurry," he confided as they drove through the rain-washed streets and parked outside a discreetly lighted tavern the name of which Sara could not make out. "At least this place is too expensive for most of the other guys to follow, so I'll have you to myself."

"Are you sure you can afford it?" Sara asked as she followed her escort into a room which was as quiet and dark as Chico's had been loud and noisy.

"I can afford it once in a while," he grinned. "I'm a big boy, now, Sara, and I earn my own money."

"I'm sure you do," she said hastily, "but well, I mean you're young and I know you've just qualified as a lawyer."

"Got my first case today." He began to talk to her about various lawsuits and Sara listened politely at first, and then with growing interest. Bobby was the first boy she had been out with who was not in any way concerned with the fashion trade and she was surprised how interesting she found him and could not believe it when she looked at her watch and saw it was past one o'clock.

"Hey, I'd better be getting back home, I have to be up early in the morning."

Reluctantly Bobby called for the bill. "One last dance while we're waiting," he said and pulled her on to the dance floor.

Dreamily they circled it together in time to a slow foxtrot, Sara's hair glowed more red than gold in the dim light and her dress swirled around her as she swayed against her partner.

It was nearly half-past one before she finally bade him goodnight and dreamily she undressed and climbed into bed. Outside in the dark sky the moon silvered the tops of the skyscrapers and a truant beam entered the window and picked out the filmy dress that lay like Cinderella's ball gown over the back of a chair.

Sara looked at it happily, seeing Marc's dark puckish face in the shadows and hearing his voice in the mournful hooting of a ship's siren far below on the

Hudson River. "Sara," he was saying, "I miss you, Sara, Come home soon."

Contrary to her expectations Sara was awake long before her usual time but when she went in to breakfast Mrs. Marriott was already seated at the table a mound of drawings in front of her.

"More schemes for the interior of the new store," she explained and passed a couple of them over to Sara who looked at them and pulled a face.

Mrs. Marriott nodded. "They're not good are they? I really am at my wit's end. If I don't find something I like soon, I'll have to copy my New York store."

"It seems impossible you can't find what you want. I always thought America was the home of interior decorating."

"We've been too good at it for too long," was the answer. "And most of the designers are getting above themselves. It's rather like Paris. At one time some of the successful designers became so over-confident that they thought they could get away with anything. They forgot they were designing for women and just created whatever came into their heads. Do you remember the balloon skirts and flat bosoms? And those dreadful Sacks. After a while the majority of women stopped buying them and the designers came down to earth pretty quickly." She tapped a finger on the drawings in front of her. "That's what'll happen to these men too."

"You really need to get hold of someone who is unspoilt, someone who is just out of Art School, perhaps?"

"It's a fallacy to think you'll find a genius that way.

It's tried and tested ones for me every time."

"The tried and tested ones aren't being very helpful at the moment, are they?" Sara said drily, and helped herself to some liver and bacon from the silver tureen on the sideboard. She gobbled it down quickly and then poured herself a cup of coffee. "Gosh, I'm ravenous."

"Late nights must agree with you. How did your evening go?"

"Very well. Bobby's a sweet boy."

"Sweet enough to make you stay here longer than three months?"

Feeling uncomfortable, Sara shook her head. "I'm sorry, but I couldn't think of it." She suddenly remembered the dress. "Marc said you had something to do with the dress. It was absolutely wonderful."

"I'm glad you liked it. He sent it to me a week ago and I kept it in my own room. I was determined not to give it to you until you were going somewhere special. That's why I was so disappointed when you kept refusing to go out."

"Well, I won't refuse any more," Sara promised. "Bobby's going to show me some of the sights. After all, I can't go back to England without having climbed to the top of the Empire State Building or taken a ride on the ferry around Staten Island."

"You certainly can't," Mrs. Marriott laughed, and gathering up her papers left the room.

They spent the week-end on Long Island as usual and many times it was on the tip of Sara's tongue to tell Mrs. Marriott she had seen her daughter. But always she managed to hold the words back, remembering her promise to Sally. Try though she had, she could not formulate a plan to bring the two women together again, and decided to let events follow a natural course, a weak way but the only one she could think of.

They returned to the city early on Monday morning and as always Sara enjoyed the long drive back. How different the Cadillac was from her father's car; there was almost no sensation of being driven and it was as if one were travelling on air, so free from bumps was the journey.

"If you'd like to learn to drive, Rogers could teach you," Mrs. Marriott said suddenly.

"I'd be scared to handle a car this size. Anyway, there's no point—I won't be able to have a car of my own for years yet."

"Lots of models over here can afford cars." Once again Sara recognised the bait and once more she refused to be drawn. Realising it Mrs. Marriott said:

"What an obstinate girl you are! Though I admire you for it in many ways." She patted her arm. "I'm getting tickets for 'The Music Man', I'd like you to come and see it with me."

"How super!" As always when she was excited Sara reverted to schoolgirl vernacular. "It was running in London when I left, but I've not managed to see it yet."

"I'm glad. We'll make a night of it and have dinner at the Persian Room."

Sara's eyes glowed and she was feeling particularly happy when she entered the store.

The day was an unusually busy one and she had to

show the Collection on six separate occasions. By the time she returned to the apartment she was so tired that she went to bed immediately after dinner.

Tuesday was a much quieter day and Sara had permission to leave the store at four o'clock. She was delighted with this for it meant she would be able to see Sally earlier than she had anticipated.

The moment she got back to the flat she changed into a skirt and jumper and put on a pair of flat-heeled shoes, then picking up a raincoat and tying a scarf over her head because the evening was gusty, she stepped out of the flat. Her hand was still on the door when Mrs. Marriott came out of the elevator.

"I didn't realise you were leaving the store earlier," she said breathlessly. "I tried to contact you but you'd already gone."

"Mrs. Banks said I could. Did another client come in then?"

"No, no. It's just that wanted to tell you about tonight. I've got the tickets for the show."

Sara stared at her discomfited.

"What's the matter?" Mrs. Marriott said sharply. "You remember I said I was getting tickets?"

"Yes, I know. But you didn't say tonight."

"Because I didn't realise myself when I'd be getting them. They're very difficult to obtain." She took in Sara's appearance. "Anyway, if you were going out like *that* you couldn't be going anywhere too important to cancel."

"But it *is* important," Sara blurted out, "and I can't cancel it."

Even as she spoke she realised that not to turn up at

Sally's when she had said she would, might irretrievably harm her relationship with the girl. It did not appear to be helping her relationship with Mrs. Marriott either at the moment, for the woman looked distinctly annoyed.

"Come, Sara, don't be childish. If you're going out with Bobby I'm sure he won't mind if—"

"I can't," Sara said quickly. "I've got to go."

"Who is it with?"

This was the question Sara had dreaded and she stared dumbly at the questioner.

"Very well," Mrs. Marriott said. "If you don't want to tell me, I understand."

Without a word she walked past Sara and entered the apartment, closing the door behind her. Yet there was a finality about it that made Sara feel uncomfortable and she hesitated. wondering whether to go in and tell Mrs. Marriott the truth. If only she had not promised Sally to keep their meeting a secret! Still, there was nothing she could do about it now and with a heavy heart she went down in the lift to the ground floor and out into the street.

CHAPTER XIV

IT was one thing to visit Sally by car and quite another proposition to go by public transport. America might be far in advance of Europe in many things, but certainly not when it came to transport. Compared with the British Underground system, New York's was antiquated, and remembering how easily one could travel from Mayfair to Balham, she fumed at the intricacies involved in going from Fifth Avenue to down-town New York.

The subway nearest the penthouse did not serve the area where Sally lived, and though, in London, changing from one line to another would have necessitated moving only to a different platform or, at the most, another trip on an escalator, in New York one had to go to an entirely different station, which necessitated coming back up into the street again, and sometimes walking a couple of blocks.

It was past seven by the time Sara arrived outside the peeling door that led into the Lamberts' tiny flat—if one room and kitchen could be designated as such.

At her knock Sally herself appeared, looking at Sara in surprise.

"So you did turn up. I wondered whether you would. Come on in. Garry's just got back and he's having a wash in our bathroom." She grinned. "It's our kitchen too, so don't go near it!"

Sara took off her coat and wandered over to look at the baby gurgling away in the carry-cot.

"I haven't fed her yet," Sally said. "I've been awfully behind-hand today, but if you'd like to do it for me . . . ."

Willingly Sara took the bottle which Sally was holding out. She bent over the cot and lowering the blankets put the bottle in the child's mouth.

"Wouldn't you like to pick her up?" Without waiting for a reply, Sally dumped the baby in Sara's arms.

Sara had never fed a baby before. She had been too young to do so when her own brother had been born and none of her friends' parents had had any young children either. All she knew of babies was what she had read in books and now, staring down at the warm, soft bundle in her arms, she was conscious of a strange stirring in her heart, a tenderness that filled her eyes and made her suddenly aware of the fact that she was a woman. One was apt to forget this when intent on a career. It was a salutory thought and she pondered on it as the baby sucked at the teat.

"What's her name?" she asked Sally as the girl busily laid the table.

"Amanda, but we call her Mandy for short." Sally set out some knives and forks, frowned at them for a moment and then hurried over to a drawer from where she took a set of raffia mats. Then she disappeared into the kitchen and there came the sound of rattling crockery and hissing water.

"I hope you're not going to any trouble because I'm here," Sara called.

Garry came out from the kitchen, freshly washed, his hair still wet.

"You're not putting us to any extra bother," he grinned. "We eat whether we have visitors or not!" He strode over and tickled the baby under her chin.

"She's a beauty, isn't she? Just like her mother."

As he talked to his little daughter, Sara studied him surreptitiously, deciding that at second sight he was even better-looking than she had remembered. No wonder Sally had fallen in love with him.

"Would you like to finish feeding your daughter?" she asked.

He nodded and with an adroitness that spoke of practice, transferred the baby into the crook of his arm. Sara walked over to a drawing-board in a corner of the room. The drawing on it depicted the interior of a bedroom and she was surprised at the sureness of the colour and the boldness of the design.

"Is this your scheme?" she asked.

"Yes. I work them out while I ride the elevator! You'd be surprised how much I've picked up just listening to the women's conversation going on around me!"

He grinned and Sara grinned back at him, but she was not concentrating on what he was saying for she had suddenly thought of a wonderful idea. How stupid not to have thought of it before!

Supper was an informal meal and though Sally had

made many deprecating remarks about her ability to
cook, there was nothing to complain of in the superb
Rissotto and delicious salad. The rolls were hot and
crisp, the cheese that came with it was fragrant and
the coffee excellent.

Garry beamed at his wife; Sally beamed back at
him and watching them Sara had no need to ask
whether they were happy.

"It beats me how you manage to cook such a meal
and go out to work at the same time," she said as she
accepted another cup of coffee. "In England I share
a flat with another girl but she does most of the
cooking."

"If you're a model you must be standing on your
feet most of the day," Sally commented. "I'd hate to
do anything like that." She looked at her hands and
wryly made a face at her broken nails. "I'm a typist
now," she admitted, "so much for all *my* work at the
Art School. Still I've no regrets about it. I wouldn't
have met Garry otherwise. But don't let's talk about
us any more, we seem to have done nothing else since
you arrived. Tell me about yourself. Do you like
working at the store? Is it different from being in a
London one? I suppose it must be quite a change from
a couturier's?"

The questions tumbled out and Sara did her best to
answer them. Yet all the while she had the feeling
that the questions uppermost in Sally's mind were
whether Sara liked living with her mother and
whether Mrs. Marriott was trying to put the English
girl in Sally's own place as a daughter.

Sara wondered how she could bring up Mrs. Marriott's name, but decided that to do so would be disastrous. Much as she wanted to hurry things forward she realised that events would have to take place in their own time and that the reconciliation she was hoping for was something that could not be hurried. The first thing to do was to gain the confidence of this couple and she would fail lamentably if they thought she was here either to spy on them or to influence them in any way.

Yet strangely enough it was Sally herself who spoke her mother's name, and she did so abruptly, almost as if the words were forced out of her.

"You didn't tell my—you didn't tell her you were coming here, did you?"

"No. You'd asked me to say nothing . . . . It was jolly awkward though. She'd got tickets for 'The Music Man' tonight and I had to refuse them."

"Oh, you silly girl. It's a fabulous show. Garry and I have been longing to see it but it's so difficult with a baby—we've no-one to leave her with in the evenings."

"I don't mind baby-sitting for you," Sara volunteered.

"That's very sweet of you, but I wouldn't dream of it."

"But I'd love to." Sara glanced at her watch. "Why, it's only half-past eight now, you'd probably have time to go to a cinema right now."

Sally looked at her husband and he looked back at her.

"No, we couldn't," the girl said. "It isn't right. You've come all this way to see us and—"

"Oh, do go out for a little while," Sara urged. "I'd love to stay alone with the baby. I only hope she cries. Then I can have a chance of picking her up and giving her a cuddle!"

Although they still maintained an outward show of reluctance, it was obvious that Sally and her husband relished the prospect of going out together, and as she put on her coat Sally confided that since the baby's arrival they had only managed to go out in the evenings on their own—something neither of them really liked.

"It's so good of you," she whispered as she followed her husband to the door. "We probably won't go to a movie—it means we'd get back too late and you've got a long journey ahead of you. But we'll just go out for a cup of coffee and a stroll round the shops."

Left alone, Sara sat down again at the table. Her eyes ranged the room, seeing its dinginess that no amount of cleaning and polishing could hide. There was no carpet on the floor and the pattern of the linoleum was almost rubbed away in patches. The gay table-mats could not hide the scarred wooden table and the chairs, though practical for sitting on, were hardly comfortable for resting in.

With a sigh she stood up and began to clear away the dishes which Sally, in her hurry to get out, had left stacked together, promising to wash them on her return. Sara carried them into the kitchen, staring round in horror at the tiny area and marvelling that anyone could produce a cup of coffee in such a place let alone a proper meal. What a far cry this was from the kitchen in the penthouse! She set to work at the sink, filling it with warm water and adding a handful of soap flakes. As she worked she sang, the latest hit to which she and Bobby had danced a few nights ago. By nine o'clock all the dishes had been put away, the kitchen tidied and the living-room-cum-bedroom swept clean with a broom which she had found behind the kitchen door.

She wandered over to the window and moving aside the curtain, looked out into the street. It was a noisy neighbourhood and cars and buses constantly chugged past. She let the curtain fall back into position again and wandered around the room, coming to a full-stop by the easel. She looked at the drawing again and picked it up to take it to the light. As she removed it she saw another sketch underneath and she stared at it, giving a whistle of surprise as she saw it was the interior for a shop.

The treatment was a modern one, yet it combined efficiency with a certain rustic charm, accentuated by the use of different coloured woods which not only formed the walls, but also the counters and ceiling. Strangely enough it did not have the heavy look she would have associated with wood, and she realised why as she saw that most of them were light veneers and all of them were used in their natural state with a high gloss polish.

She began to look through all the other drawings, seeing that many of them were lay-outs for a department store. How strange for Garry to be doing this sort of thing. Had he heard that Mrs. Marriott was looking for a designer? Suddenly something went click in her mind. Garry was just the type of designer

Mrs. Marriott was looking for! She swung round and in her excitement the drawings fell to the floor. As she bent to pick them up she saw that a small newspaper cutting had fluttered out from beneath one of them and she picked it up and read it. It was a cutting from a New York paper saying that Marriott's of Fifth Avenue were opening another branch and that various leading decorators were being called in to submit specifications. There was no doubt that Garry had seen this and had toyed with the idea of submitting something himself. Or at least if he had not actually intended to submit it, it had certainly fired him into creating something of his own.

Sara set the drawings on the table in front of her and studied them carefully. Two of them were designs for Executive offices one was for the interior of a general floor and the other was for the fashion department. The last drawing she looked at was the one she liked best, for it showed the entrance to the store itself. She did not know how far advanced Mrs. Marriott's plans were but she could not imagine that any of them could beat this one. It was simplicity itself, the beauty of it being in the elegant curves of the staircase leading to the first floor and gallery. The gallery, as far as Sara could make out, was intended as a display hall, with concealed lighting and groups of chairs carefully situated near each counter. This was obviously the place where customers could arrange to meet one another, where they could sit and rest between purchases and feast their eyes on all the lovely things available in the store.

She knew that in New York itself it would not have

been a practical proposition, for as Mrs. Marriott had said, property was so expensive that one could not afford to waste even an inch of it. But on Long Island there was no doubt that such a scheme could be carried out, and almost without thinking she picked up four or five of the drawings and rolled them together, securing them with a rubber band which she found lying beneath the easel.

Guiltily she stared down at the rolled package in her hand. She did not need to ask herself what she was going to do with it. She knew! There were voices outside, Garry's deep one and Sally's lighter, more buoyant tone. Not giving herself a chance to change her mind, Sara stuffed the drawings into a pocket of her raincoat and then draped the coat carefully back over the chair.

When the young couple came in she was sitting demurely in a chair looking at a magazine.

"How did you enjoy your stroll?" she asked.

"It was fabulous," Sally said. "You're an angel to baby-sit for us."

"Any time you like," Sara said and conscious of her raincoat, she stood up. "I'd better be going. I'm not sure of my way and—"

"I'll walk you to the subway," Garry said and reached out to help her on with her coat.

Before he could do so, Sara darted across and pulled it from the chair, aware of his surprised glance as she put it on and buttoned it up quickly.

"I've got a thing about people helping me on with my coat," she explained. "It's a sort of superstition!"

Although it was midnight when she returned to the penthouse, the lights were still on in the living-room and after leaving her coat in the bedroom, Sara apprehensively went in to see her hostess. The woman was sitting on the settee surrounded by papers and blueprints. She did not look up as Sara came in and, realising she was asleep, she tip-toed forward and looked at the relaxed face, seeing the tired droop to the mouth and the waxy pallor of the skin beneath the carefully applied make-up. Mrs. Marriott might not show her age nor her responsibilities when she was awake, but in sleep she could not hide them.

Slowly Sara bent and tidied all the papers into a neat pile. She was just placing them on the settee when she felt her scalp tingle. Here was the opportunity she was looking for.

Quickly she hurried back to her bedroom, the blueprints still clutched in her hand. On the bed lay Garry's designs and she picked them up and was just going to insert them amongst those in her hand when she stopped. Picking up her bag she took out a pencil and feverishly scrawled a name at the bottom of each of Garry's designs. Then not giving herself time to change her mind she put them at the bottom of the pile and tip-toed back to the living-room.

Mrs. Marriott was still asleep and Sara crept across the carpet and placed the papers around her feet again. She had just straightened when Mrs. Marriott's eyelids fluttered and she opened her eyes.

"Oh there you are Sara. I must have dropped off to sleep."

"I'm sorry if I awakened you, but I couldn't go to

bed until I'd spoken to you. I want to apologise about tonight."

"You don't owe me an apology, I owe *you* one. I'd no right to ask you to break a date in order to come out with me."

"I—I'd have broken any date with any boy in the world rather than let you down," Sara said impulsively. "But this one was so special . . . Oh please, Mrs. Marriott, do believe me."

"My dear child, don't get so upset over it. Of course I believe you. If you can't tell me who it was with . . ."

"I'll tell you one day," Sara promised. "But at the moment I'd like to keep it a secret."

"A secret?" The blue eyes were speculative. "You never struck me as the sort of girl to keep secrets, Sara. You're not doing anything of which you're ashamed, are you?"

"No—it's nothing like that. I'll be able to tell you soon, but at the moment I can't."

Mrs. Marriott appeared satisfied with this somewhat lame excuse and she patted Sara's cheek. "All right, child. Stop looking so worried and go to bed. I've just got to look at a few more papers then I'll be following you."

"Don't you think you've done enough for tonight?" Sara asked, but Mrs. Marriott did not answer and bent to pick up the drawings around her feet. Sara longed to wait until she came upon Garry's but she knew that if she did so her face would give her away and she was determined not to tell Mrs. Marriott who had done the drawings until the woman had had a chance to look at them with an unbiased gaze.

Murmuring goodnight she returned to her bedroom and began to undress, but as she lay in bed sleep was a long way away and every beat of her heart echoed the question in her mind: "Would Mrs. Marriott find Garry's designs acceptable, or would she hate them as she had hated all the others she had seen?"

CHAPTER XV

IN the morning Mrs. Marriott made no reference to
the drawings and Sara could hardly hide her disappointment as they breakfasted together. Eager to
prolong the meeting in the hope that something
would be said, she accepted an offer of a lift to work
instead of walking, which she usually did. But even
as they rode down Fifth Avenue Mrs. Marriott said
nothing and in desperation, knowing she could not
work through the day without finding out what had
happened, Sara brought up the subject herself.

"What drawings?" Mrs. Marriott asked.

"The ones you were looking at when I came in last
night."

"Oh those." The vivid blue eyes closed for a
moment. "I'm afraid I didn't do any work after all. I
was so tired after you left that I went to bed myself.
But I've got them with me and I'll look at them in the
office."

"I wonder if you'll like them? I mean, it'd be marvellous if you found some designs that you thought
were absolutely smashing."

Mrs. Marriott looked at her in surprise. "It certainly would. But I'm hardly likely to at this stage. They're going from bad to worse and I've almost made up my mind to copy the decor I've already got. There's a lot to be said for grey and pink."

"But you don't want the same," Sara protested. "I mean—"

The car drew to a stop outside the main entrance and she jumped out, knowing that if she said anymore she would give the game away. During the rest of the morning she was too busy to think about anything other than the Donnell Collection for there were appointments booked for every single hour. Never had she modelled so long at one stretch and by mid-day the smile on her face was taut and she felt that unless she took off her shoes and rested with her feet up, she would faint.

"I feel as if I'm in training for the Olympics," she murmured as Mrs. Banks came into the dressing-room to help her change from one outfit into another. "Is the afternoon as bad?"

"Luckily no. I'm sorry about this morning, Sara, but I was away yesterday and my assistant booked all these clients without realising there's only you to do the modelling."

"Oh well," Sara said as cheerfully as she could, "it's a good thing to know that even American Efficiency fails sometimes!"

At lunchtime she was too tired to go to the canteen and decided to rest for half-an-hour and manage with a cup of coffee and a sandwich at the local drug store. Sara liked the drug stores for they had an easy-going atmosphere that reminded her of a village shop. One could buy almost anything in the average American drug store she had found; apart from medicine and cosmetics there was generally a long counter serving all sorts of sandwiches and snacks and drinks. And then there were books to buy, records to choose and a hundred and one different items from cups and saucers to cardigans. In fact as far as she could see, drug stores were almost competing with Woolworth's!

She bent and rubbed her toes, stretching them backwards and forwards to ease the cramp.

"Who was it said that you became a cripple if you wore high-heels all the time?" she wondered aloud.

"Whoever it was he knew a thing or two." A voice spoke behind her and she swung round to see Mrs. Marriott in the doorway.

She jumped to her feet in surprise. "Is anything the matter? Are you looking for Mrs. Banks?"

"No, I'm looking for you. I want to talk to you." Mrs. Marriott came further into the room and motioned her to sit down.

With a vague presentiment of something wrong, Sara did as she was told.

"Sara, I want you to answer me truthfully. Half-an-hour ago I was looking through those drawings—the ones you found me working on last night. When I looked at them this morning I found some different ones there."

"D-different ones?" Sara asked innocently.

"Yes. I'd looked at those drawings pretty carefully last night, and I distinctly remember there were ten of them. This morning there are fifteen." From the portfolio she was carrying, Mrs. Marriott drew out the five drawings which Sara had inserted. "Here they are—and I'd like to know where they came from. I think you can supply the answer."

"Why me?" Sara asked, desperately playing for time.

"Because I'm pretty sure you put them there. Now come, Sara, I'm not a fool. You acted very strangely about the whole thing this morning."

Miserably aware that her employer was too astute to be fooled any longer, Sara nodded.

"You're quite right," she mumbled. "I—I did put them there."

"I thought so. Would you kindly tell me where they came from?"

"Could you tell me first of all whether you— whether you liked them?"

Mrs. Marriott's face gave nothing away and her mouth was a thin, firm line. "Tell me first where you got them."

Realising there was no bargain to be made, Sara did so.

"Well, I—well, that's where I went last night. I told you I didn't have a date and—and I didn't. Not a proper date, I mean. I met this young man. He's an interior decorator although he's working as an elevator boy right now. I was sure he could do what you wanted, but it seemed pointless my telling you about him because I didn't think you'd believe me." She stopped and looked at Mrs. Marriott but the woman's face still gave nothing away. "I mean if this—if this young man was already working as an interior decorater there might have been some point in my telling you about him, but you wouldn't have wanted to see his drawings if I'd told you he was operating a lift, would you?"

"Probably not," came the dry reply. "One doesn't normally associate elevator boys with interior decorating."

"But everybody has to start somewhere," Sara protested.

"Then let him start in an Architect's office," Mrs. Marriott retorted. "There must be something wrong with him if he can't get a job. Or isn't he properly trained?"

"Oh yes, he's properly trained. But he—but he doesn't like working with the people who've offered him jobs. He's got his own ideas and—"

"A rebel, I suppose? Well, I can't blame him for that. When I started Marriott's *my* ideas were considered outlandish too."

"Do you consider those drawing of his outlandish?" Sara asked boldly.

"No I don't. They're different admittedly, but it's a difference I like. The young man doesn't know many of the things I wish to have incorporated, but once he did I'm sure he'd be able to come up with something I approved of."

"Do you mean you'll give him a chance to do the work for you?" Sara gasped.

"Well, I'd like to see more of his designs, but from what I've already seen I'd say he stands a good chance. Do you think you could bring him to see me?"

This was the question Sara had been dreading. If she were to tell Mrs. Marriott that the person in question was her son-in-law would she refuse to meet him? But how could she bring him without first warning her? And even if Mrs. Marriott agreed to see Garry, would Garry agree to see Mrs. Marriott? This was something she had not even considered until now, and as it entered her mind Sara felt all her rising hopes sink despondently.

"I'll have to—to talk to him first," she stammered. "He's a v-very odd—a very difficult young man—and—"

"Go and talk to him at once! I like his drawings, Sara, and if he'll co-operate with me, I'm pretty sure I can use him. A rebel he might be, but he's got to toe *some* lines sooner or later. Tell him I want to see him right away!"

"But he works an elevator," Sara pleaded.

"I'll see him this evening then. You can bring him to the apartment. Now go off and find him. I'll tell Gina you won't be back until later this afternoon."

As she gathered up her coat and raced down to the street, Sara was elated that at least part of her plan had worked. The most important part! Mrs. Marriott liked Garry's drawings. All she had to do now was to bring the two of them together. She could not believe he would refuse, particularly when he realised he would be given the opportunity of doing the work for which he had been trained. And what a wonderful opportunity it would be to design a new store, to gain a commission which other important decorators had failed to win!

She was busy formulating exactly what she was going to say to him as she rode in the bus down to Forty-

Second Street. Jumping off at the corner she ran as fast as she could along the busy thoroughfare, weaving in and out of shoppers until she reached Macy's. Thank goodness she had remembered Garry worked here. Breathlessly she pushed her way into the store and looked round for the elevators. There seemed to be hundreds of them but none of the attendants looked like Garry and she was beginning to wonder whether she had made a mistake after all when the last elevator in the line came down and as the doors slid back a tall, good-looking man stepped to one side.

"Garry!" She darted forward and he stared at her in surprise.

"Sara, what on earth are you doing here?"

"I've come to see you. I've got to talk to you."

"Can't it wait till later?" He looked at some women coming towards him and stepped into the lift.

"What time are you off for lunch?" she whispered.

"I've already had it and it's my late night tonight. I don't finish until nine."

"Oh dear, it's terribly important." Behind her women jostled to get into the elevator and Sara, unwilling to let Garry disappear again, stepped in too. The lift doors closed and they glided up to the next floor.

"Do you think you could get a couple of hours off?" she murmured under cover of his monotonous chanting of the goods available on each floor.

"Lingerie, linen and all ladies' wear—I'm afraid it's impossible," he mumbled all in one breath.

"But it's important I tell you. Those drawings of yours—Mrs. Marriott loved them."

"What?" In his excitement Garry forgot where he was and turned round sharply. His elbow jerked against the elevator handle and the doors opened and closed and then opened again, almost wedging a woman in between them.

"What the heck's the matter with you?" the irate customer grumbled. "Can't you give me a chance to get out before closing the doors?"

"I'm terribly sorry, ma'am," Garry apologised. "It was an accident."

Slightly mollified by the engaging smile he flashed at her, the woman went off and Garry mopped his brow.

"Look Sara, I can't talk to you now. I'll end up getting fired if I do."

"It won't matter if you *are* fired! That's what I'm trying to tell you. Mrs. Marriott loves your drawings. I took them last night when you and Sally were out. I know I should have asked you first, but I was afraid that if I did you'd say No."

"You're darn right I would. I didn't do those drawings for Mrs. Marriott to see."

"Then what were you doing them for? You read in one of the newspapers that she was opening a new store. There's no point denying it," she said defiantly, "because I saw the cutting."

He had the grace to redden. "I was doing them for my own benefit. I'd no intention of sending them to her—or anybody else."

"More fool you then," Sara said, "or do you want to ride in an elevator all your life?"

He looked about to make an angry retort but more

customers came into the lift and by the time he had
taken them to the Ground Floor his temper had abated
and he was prepared to admit the truth of Sara's last
remark.

"O.K. Sara, you win. What am I supposed to do
now?"

"Mrs. Marriott wants to see you. She says you don't
know all the things she's got planned for the new
store so that the way your designs stand right now,
they're no good."

"Of course they're no good," he said impatiently.
"They're just rough sketches. The whole thing would
have to be drawn to scale and—"

"I know," Sara intervened, anxious to finish what
she had to before any more customers came in, and
not relishing the prospect of riding up and down in an
elevator much longer. "The question is, can you get
any time off to come and see her?"

"No. It'll have to be this evening about ten. I'm sure
my mother-in-law can manage to stay up until then!"

He leaned against the side of the wall and Sara
could not help noticing how handsome he looked in
his uniform, with its tight-fitting grey trousers and
short jacket with countless brass buttons.

He saw her glance and scowled, looking if anything
even more handsome.

"Don't stare at me in this monkey-suit. It's the one
thing I hate about the job."

"You look fine," she giggled. "No wonder Sally fell
in love with you."

"She didn't see me like this. At Art School I had a
beard and paint-stained corduroys!"

The mention of Art School suddenly reminded him of the real position between himself and Mrs. Marriott, a position which he had forgotten in his excitement at Sara's news.

"She does know it's *me*, doesn't she?" he asked anxiously. "I mean you haven't been spinning her some yarn about who I am, have you?" As he looked at Sara's face he knew the answer and his expression grew grim. "Look here, I've no intention of presenting myself to Mrs. Marriott unless she knows exactly who she's going to see."

"But does she know you? I mean, has she ever met you before?"

"She saw me once—the first time I called to take Sally out. She was charming to me because she'd no idea that Sally was serious about me. Once she learned *that*, I wasn't allowed to set foot in the apartment!"

"Well, if she only saw you once she wouldn't remember you," Sara said, deliberately misunderstanding him. "And anyway, you had a beard then."

"That's got nothing to do with it! I tell you I've no intention of talking to her about my designs unless she knows who I am."

"But why? She won't take your designs just because you're her son-in-law."

"That's for sure! But she might *not* take them for that reason."

"All the more necessity not to tell her who you are," Sara pleaded. "Oh Garry, this is the chance you've been waiting for. If you do the interior décor for the new store and it's a success, you'll have open sesame to every big firm in the country. You'll be able to take a job and name your own price. You can't turn down a chance like that."

"I can and I will," he said grimly. "I don't need any favours from my mother-in-law."

"But she wouldn't be giving you any favours. I tell you she likes your work and wants to talk to you about it."

"No. I won't see her until you tell her who I am. That's final."

"Oh you men!" Sara said furiously. "You've all got the same beastly pride. You're as bad as Sally and she's got much more reason to be angry with her mother than you have."

"Is that so?" he said mutinously. "Mrs. Marriott said some pretty nasty things about me."

"And you'd say some pretty nasty things about a penniless young man who wanted to marry *your* daughter," Sara retorted. "Even if you're still an elevator boy when you're sixty-five, you won't relish the prospect of her eloping with a penniless nobody. And that's what you were whether you like it or not."

Garry's eyes flashed with anger but Sara stared at him defiantly, the tension leaving her body as she saw him suddenly relax.

"You've got an uncanny habit of hitting where it hurts most," he admitted. "Six months ago I'd have knocked anyone down for saying that. But today, with a baby of my own, I realise a lot of things I never realised before."

"Well then, come and see Mrs. Marriott. If she agrees to give you the commission there's no reason why you can't finish the job and then tell her who you are. By that time I'm sure you'll be getting on with her famously and it'll only be a matter of a little more persuasion to get Sally to talk to her mother too."

"You're a curious girl," Garry said slowly. "Why are you so keen on getting Sally and her mother back again?"

"Because it isn't right for them to be estranged. I'm not awfully close to my mother now, yet when I'm upset or worried she's the first person I'd turn to. I'm sure that would apply to Sally."

"She went through quite a lot of trouble with the baby," he said grimly, "and she managed pretty well without her mother. As long as I'm here to take care of her—"

"Say something happens to you? What would happen to Sally then?"

It was an unpalatable thought and he pushed it away. "You're an awkward little customer, aren't you? Always asking questions that are better left unsaid."

"That's what my father says to me," she smiled. "Look Garry, come straight to the apartment when you finish here tonight. I'll be waiting at the door for you."

"O.K.," he murmured. "But I'm still not sure I'm doing the right thing."

"You *are* doing the right thing," she reiterated. "Believe me, you are!"

CHAPTER XVI

SARA was too excited to eat any dinner that evening and she did no more than push the food around the plate. At one moment she was sure her plan would work, and the next she was convinced it was doomed to failure. What would happen if Mrs. Marriott recognised her son-in-law after all? Would she throw him out? Would they have a fight? And if she didn't recognise him, what would happen then?

Sara tried to visualise Garry and his mother-in-law discussing different decorative schemes, amicably deciding what they were going to do and how they were going to do it. Her mind raced ahead to a month's time and further blue-prints and discussions, with Garry on much more familiar terms with Mrs. Marriott and Mrs. Marriott admitting to Sara how much she liked the interior decorator.

It was then that Sara would tell her who Garry was. How happy Mrs. Marriott would be. The look of joy on her face—

"What's the matter with you, Sara?"

Sara lifted her head with a jerk. "I'm sorry, was I doing anything wrong?"

"Not wrong, my dear, you were just sitting there mumbling to yourself. Do you feel all right?"

"Yes, perfectly."

"Then you're nervous about this friend of yours, I suppose? You've nothing to worry about, I told you I liked his ideas and I'm sure we'll get on well together. Now try to eat your dinner. It's a pity to waste good food."

Sara did as she was told but it was an effort and the fish, delicious though it was, stuck in her throat, while the soufflé, melting sugary mouthfuls, was as tasteless as if it were yesterday's cold potatoes.

She was grateful when, dinner over, they retired to the drawing-room and Mrs. Marriott picked up the inevitable bundle of papers to study as Sara turned on the television and looked at a coloured Spectacular, careful to keep the volume low. Frequently she looked at her watch and once held it to her ear to make sure it was still going. At last the hands pointed to nine-thirty. Garry should be here any minute. She stood up and walked to the door.

"Where are you going, Sara?"

"I'm going to meet—" she hesitated, her breath exhaling slowly as she tried to remember what name she had scribbled on the drawings. Disastrous to call Garry by one name if she'd written down another! Fate came to her aid as it always seemed to do and Mrs. Marriott looked at her and smiled.

"Really, Sara, this Gerald of yours can find his way up to the apartment without your going down for him."

Gerald! That was it! Sara drew a sigh of relief. How stupid of her to have forgotten.

"He's very nervous," she mumbled, "and I promised I'd meet him outside."

She hurried out, but as she reached the elevator she saw it was already on their floor and the doors swung back to disclose Garry. He was wearing a dark-grey suit, the one he had worn when she had had supper with him and his wife. Probably the only one he possessed other than his elevator uniform. His hair was brushed down slickly and his face was unusually pale.

"Hullo Sara. I nearly didn't come."

"There's nothing to worry about."

Not giving him a chance to change his mind she pulled him into the apartment and closed the door. Still keeping her hand on his arm she led the way down the hall into the living-room. Seeing it with his eyes she could well imagine how great a contrast he must find it compared with his own flat, and guessed that he was wondering how he had ever had the temerity to take Sally from a place like this.

Mrs. Marriott had no idea of any of the thoughts racing through the minds of either of the young people in front of her and she stood up and came forward.

"So you're Gerald," she smiled. "Come in and sit down."

Garry looked at Sara in puzzlement and then followed Mrs. Marriott further into the living-room. He sat on the edge of the settee, poised as if ready for flight, but Mrs. Marriott appeared not to notice and picked up his drawings which she had placed on a table beside her.

"These are good," she said, "and you should thank Sara for having the intelligence to show them to me."

"I'd no idea she was going to do it," he said jerkily. "She took them without my knowledge. She knew I'd never show them to you."

"I don't see why, they're excellent. Where did you train?"

He mentioned the name of his Art School and for a moment Mrs. Marriott's mouth tightened. Then she continued to speak, asking him pertinent questions about his work and ideas.

Once he began talking about his work Garry lost his inhibitions, and Sara could well see what it was that had attracted Sally to him—apart from the fact that he was so handsome. She was the first to admit that looks were the weakest reason for marrying someone; similarity of outlook and interests, a basic belief in the same things were much more important. When talking about his work Garry was neither humorous nor casual, for he believed wholeheartedly in all the theories he was expounding and was determined that one day he would put those theories into practice and prove that he was right.

"Colour is a great force—we're just beginning to realise quite what it can do but we're still afraid to tap it."

"Tap it?" Mrs. Marriott asked puzzled.

"Yes. A great many efficiency experts recommend the use of colour in the design of factories. They've found that workers produce more if they're wearing gaily-coloured uniforms rather than drab ones. They also know that workers manipulating extremely noisy machines found the noise less disturbing when the machines were painted grey or lilac instead of being left in the original brown or black."

"How interesting," Mrs. Marriott said. "You're quite right, of course. I've read about it. I suppose that's one of the reasons they use white and green in hospitals."

"Exactly. White looks virginal and pure—aseptic in other words—while green is soothing." Garry's voice dipped lower and became full of portent. "But have you ever thought *why* colours have this effect?"

"No. I can't say I have. Beyond the fact that there's a lot of chlorophyll in green—that's *why* it's green!"

"Chlorophyll is just a word that scientists have given to something that's been going on for centuries. But it doesn't tell you what that colour does. In fact, I believe that every single colour has a vibration of its own. We all know the healing value of ultra-violet colour rays, of infra-red rays and of X-rays, but we're just beginning to learn the valuable properties of all the other colours."

His hostess seemed taken aback by the strangeness of all he was propounding.

"I've never heard anyone say this before. It's a novel theory if nothing else."

"I agree with it," Sara interrupted, and put her hand to her mouth. "I'm sorry, I shouldn't have said anything."

"Why not?" Mrs. Marriott smiled. "You needn't stand on ceremony. What were you going to say?"

"Merely that I find blue means a great deal to me. Whenever I feel depressed I surround myself with blue. And yet my Mother used to tell me it was a depressing colour."

"That's an old wives' tale," Garry put in. "Blue is the colour of the sky—the heavens. And it's also the colour we associate with the Madonna. That's why it has come to mean a healing and calming colour. A great many faith-healers use a blue light in their room when they do their work."

"All this is certainly interesting," the older woman said, "and I suppose you're going to tell me your choice of colour in your designs is based on these theories?"

"Exactly. Red is the colour exuding great energy, but on its own in a shop it will only confuse the customer and excite them. Green is the colour of the life force itself; it's the colour of revitalisation. So add a touch of green with your red and you'll have your customers in a buying mood without their being excitable or over-anxious." Garry paused and rubbed his hand across his face. "I'm sorry for going on like this."

"You've no need to be. I like hearing it." Mrs. Marriott picked up a pad and pencil and passed it over to him. "Maybe you'd like to take down some notes. I'd like to tell you some of my ideas on the new store and give you a chance to think them over tonight. In the morning I'd like you to meet my architects and see the actual blue-prints."

"I'm afraid I can't manage the morning, or any time

during the day," Garry said regretfully. "I work."

"I know you do, but I'm hoping to persuade you to change your job," Mrs. Marriott reached for a cigarette. "It's ridiculous for you to go on riding an elevator. You've a lot of talent and it's time it was put to use."

"Do you mean you're going to get me a job?"

"No, I'm not. I wouldn't recommend you to any of the interior decorators I've so far had to deal with. I feel you should start on your own. With my new store as your first commission, you'll be able to keep yourself going for quite a while. And long before it's finished you'll have other orders coming in."

Garry looked dazed by the prospect and realising how he must be feeling, Mrs. Marriott walked over to the window and stared out into the darkness, giving him a chance to compose himself. Sara stood by her side. Never had she imagined that this meeting would go as well as it had. If only Sally were here now!

Behind them Garry cleared his throat and they heard the creak of the settee as he stood up.

"Mrs. Marriott," his voice was unexpectedly loud in the silent room, and both Sara and the older woman turned to look at him. "Mrs. Marriott," he repeated, his face pale, his hands clenched at his side. "Your offer is a so generous one that I'm completely bowled over by it. But I—but I can't accept it."

"Why not? Your future is assured. There's nothing to worry about. If you're afraid that I'll go back on my word—"

"It isn't that at all. I'm sure you mean everything you say, but I—I can't take advantage of you by accepting it."

"What do you mean, take advantage of me?"

Sara took a step forward, as if by doing so she could prevent Garry from speaking, but he looked at her and shook his head.

"No, Sara, I've got to say it. I thought I could keep quiet, but I can't." He moved closer to Mrs. Marriott until only a chair stood between them. "First of all I'd like you to know this wasn't a put-up job between Sara and me. She saw my drawings and she took them on a spur of the moment decision. When you said you liked them she decided to go the whole hog and bring me here."

"I don't know why you're saying all this." Mrs. Marriott was mystified. "I know that the whole thing was Sara's idea, but that's got nothing to do with your work."

"Yes, it has. When I first came here I had made up my mind to accept whatever you offered. I was going to do the decorative schemes and lay-out for your store and then, when you were pleased with what I'd done, when you were grateful for my help, I was going to tell you who I was. But I guess I'm not cut out to do it that way. I thought my work was so important that I'd take any opportunity to get ahead. I find now that I can't."

Mrs. Marriott was shaking, the diamond brooch pinned to the bodice of her gown flashing in a thousand points of light. "What are you trying to tell me? Who *are* you?"

"Your son-in-law. Garry Lambert!"

Mrs. Marriott made no reply and Garry turned back to the settee and picked up his drawings. Sara hurried over to him and he patted her cheek.

"I'm sorry," he said huskily, "I didn't want to let you down and I didn't want to let Sal down either. But I—but I couldn't pretend."

He walked across the room and Sara's eyes blurred with tears. She blinked them away and when she looked up again he had gone.

CHAPTER XVII

MRS. MARRIOTT walked over to the settee and sat down. Beneath the light of a standard lamp she looked waxy pale and old.

"Fetch him back," she said, and though her voice was shaking it was resolute.

Not daring to question her, Sara sped across the room and along the hall. Garry was half-way out of the door and even after she told him to come back, he remained irresolute.

"Oh come *on*," she pleaded. "Don't just stand there!"

Without a word he returned to the living-room and Mrs. Marriott waved him to the chair opposite.

"You say that Sara took the drawings without asking your permission?"

"Yes I did," Sara said before he could reply. "I went to see your daughter last week and then again the other night. That's why I couldn't come with you to 'The Music Man'. I told you I had a date I couldn't break. Well, it was with Sally. I had supper with them and then they went out for a walk. When I was alone I looked at the easel—" She flung out her hands. "The rest you know."

"I see." Mrs. Marriott looked at Garry. "I appreciate your telling me what you did. I'm not sure that in your position I would have done the same. You could have accepted my offer of a job and you could have told me who you were at a time to suit yourself. I really—I really am most agreeably surprised that you didn't."

"So am I," he admitted. "I've disliked you for such a long while, Mrs. Marriott and yet talking to you like this, finding you so receptive—well I realised I couldn't go through with it."

Momentarily Mrs. Marriott closed her eyes and when she opened them again they were bright with unshed tears. "How is my daughter?"

"She's very well. She misses you but she's too obstinate to come and tell you so."

"She's not her mother's daughter for nothing," Mrs. Marriott said drily. "How have you—" she hesitated. "How have you managed to live all this while?"

"Sally and I both work. We don't live like this," he said with a slight smile, "but we get along all right."

"I never thought you would. I suppose you know why I was opposed to your marrying my daughter?"

"Yes, Sally told me. I don't blame you for thinking what you did, I guess I might have done the same in your position. If you'd told Sally that you wouldn't let her marry me until I'd proved myself—until I'd shown an ability to work and that I could hold down a job, I wouldn't have got so het-up about the whole thing. But it was your refusal even to meet me and to discuss anything that made me so mad that I persuaded Sally to elope with me."

"I shouldn't think you had to do much persuading," his mother-in-law said drily. "Sally was very much in love with you. It was probably that factor as much as any other that made me resent you."

"Resent me?" he said in surprise. "But I had nothing you could be jealous of."

"You had my daughter's love."

Garry turned brick-red and Sara, finding this emotional post-mortem somewhat overwhelming, decided to steer the conversation round to something which she considered much more important.

"Now you know who Garry is, what are you going to do, Mrs. Marriott?"

"It doesn't only depend on me. It depends on my son-in-law."

Garry looked at the woman uncertainly. "I don't know what you mean."

"It's quite simple. I made you an offer of a job and you said you couldn't accept it. I'm hoping you'll change your mind."

Garry seemed unable to take it in, and Mrs. Marriott came over to him. "I'm asking you to forgive me for having been so biased about you. I hope you'll give me a chance to show how sorry I am and—"

"I'm the one who needs to apologise," he said. "When I think of the nerve I had in dating a girl like Sal I'm not surprised you thought me a fortune hunter!"

"I don't think you're that *now*," his mother-in-law replied. "I consider you very rich—in talent. Money of your own will soon follow, believe me."

Feeling de trop, Sara left the room; what passed

between Mrs. Marriott and her son-in-law was not for other ears to hear.

She was sitting on the bed, feeling desperately and unexpectedly homesick, when Mrs. Marriott knocked on the door and came in. How different she looked! There was a luminosity about her face, a spring to her step that took years off her age.

"Garry's taking me to see Sally," she said. "We're leaving now. I thought you'd like to come."

"It's sweet of you to suggest it, but I'll feel in the way."

"Nonsense. I want you with me. If it hadn't been for you . . ." Tears filled the blue eyes. "Please my dear, come with me."

Long afterwards Sara was to remember the drive down to the poorer section of the city, and the sight of Sally's face when she opened the door of her one-roomed flat and saw the mink coated figure of her mother standing there. It had taken a lot of excited talk and interruption of one another to explain why Garry and Mrs. Marriott were together, and Sara had been hugged alternately by both the women who loudly declared her the heroine of the occasion.

But none of the joy of re-union was anything compared with the rapture with which Mrs. Marriott greeted her grandchild.

"Do you mean you've got a baby?" she gasped, her face taking on the melted look which Sara had noticed before on the faces of her mother or older relatives when babies were mentioned.

"Yes," Sally said tremulously. "A little girl. She's three months old."

"A little girl! Where is she? I must see her."

Sally drew her mother over to the carry-cot on the divan and, as if realising she was being seen by her grandmother for the first time, Mandy awoke. Large blue eyes stared into ones so similar that the relationship was obvious, and a fat, starfish-pink hand reached out in time-honoured gesture to grab the necklace that dangled enticingly within its grasp.

"Glug glug," said Mandy.

"Oh you darling!" her grandmother breathed, and without another word picked her up and cuddled her close.

"This sort of scene is all right for you women," Garry whispered to Sara. "You can cry without feeling ashamed! But us men . . . Come on, let's go and make some coffee."

Together they went into the kitchen and while Sara brewed the coffee, Garry placed cups and saucers on a tray.

"The one thing I'll always remember about America," she said as she filled the cups, "is it's coffee. It just isn't the same in England."

"I've heard lots of English people say that. I guess it's something to do with the water."

Garry picked up the tray and took it into the other room where Sally and her mother were sitting on the divan, the baby between them.

Sara did not know what had passed between mother and daughter, but whatever it was they both seemed content. There was one thing to be said for families, Sara thought as she sipped her coffee and nibbled a cookie—an American term for a biscuit—no

matter how bitter the arguments, once a reconciliation had taken place it was as if the quarrel had never
existed. Strange that this rarely applied with one's
friends.

"Blood is thicker than water after all," she said out
loud and Mrs. Marriott and Sally laughed.

"It certainly is," said the older woman. "There are
times when nothing is more apt than a cliché!"

Sara and Mrs. Marriott did not leave the flat until
well past one o'clock. But they were both too excited
to feel tired and even when they reached the penthouse they remained in the living-room talking.

"Having a baby's made Sally realise a great many
things," her mother said as she wandered round the
room, picking up an object and putting it down again.
"She knows now how easy it is to become obsessive
over a child, to want them to do as you say simply
because you feel you know better."

"Why do parents always think they know better?"
Sara asked plaintively.

"Because they generally do! Even now I don't
think I was wrong in objecting to Garry."

"But you don't object to him now, do you?" Sara
asked anxiously.

"No, no. I'm going to enjoy having him as a son-in-
law. It's been a responsibility running Marriott's on
my own, and I've a feeling he'll take a load off my
shoulders."

In this Mrs. Marriott was proved right, for during
the weeks that followed events moved so quickly that
Sara, used though she was to American hustle, found
it difficult to absorb all the changes.

Resisting the temptation to offer money, Mrs. Marriott merely gave Garry a long term contract and made no comment when he decided to buy a small house near the Long Island one. Sally and the baby could stay there, he said, and he would commute into New York each day.

"What'll happen when you work late?" Mrs. Marriott asked.

"I'll spend the night in town," he grinned. "Providing my mother-in-law will offer me house-room!"

Seeing Garry tease Mrs. Marriott, Sara had no fears for their relationship and realised that the woman's intuition had been right when she had said that in welcoming Garry as her son-in-law she was also welcoming a son.

As the days lengthened and the weather acquired that warm crispness only associated with New York in Spring, Sara began to count the days until her return home. The Donnell Collection had met with more success than anyone had anticipated, though Mrs. Marriott felt that a visit from Marc himself would produce even greater results.

"He'll be taken up by every Matron in town," she had said speculatively, "and he's bound to be a hit with them."

"Provided they don't bore him. Once Marc's bored he's unpredictable."

"Then he'll have to bring you with him! I should imagine you're the one person who can control him."

Diplomatically Sara said nothing, though she made a mental note to report this conversation to Marc when she saw him again.

When she saw him again. Only ten days now. And what hectic days they were; filled with parties, with trips to Long Island, with excursions with Bobby Walker and the buying of the inevitable presents. But at last she had completed them: nylon lingerie for Betsy and Beryl and Mrs. Fielding, a set of exquisite costume jewellery for her mother, and gay pullovers for her father and brother. In fact, looking at these last two purchases as she packed them the night before her departure she was dubious as to her selection, and wondered how they would look in the environs of Frimpton. Peter was the easiest person for whom to buy a gift: almost any gadget for his camera being acceptable. But Marc presented the greatest worry, and it was on Bobby's suggestion that she visited one of the antique shops along Lexington Avenue and discovered an exquisite jade statuette of a figure dancing. It bore a resemblance to Marc himself, having the same graceful quality and faun-like strength.

The model taking over from Sara at the store was another English girl, and Sara was delighted to learn she had trained at the Lena Lane Model School some three years earlier.

"You didn't have to train with Lydia's niece, Nina," Sara remarked.

"No, I didn't but I've heard she was a real horror. She was working with Paul Gerard until a little while ago," the girl went on, "but now she's back in London."

Sara felt a prickle of unease at the thought of Nina and herself in the same city again. But not wishing to gossip she changed the subject and they spent the rest of their meeting discussing Donnell clothes and the difference between modelling for an American audience and a British one.

"You can show the clothes at a quicker pace here," Sara advised, "and they like you to look haughty."

To Sara's surprise her departure elicited a mention in the Press and when they reached Idlewild Airport there was a battery of photographers to meet her. No wonder Mrs. Marriott had insisted on her travelling home in a Donnell suit!

All the family came to bid her goodbye and Sally had even brought the baby.

"You won't forget to let us know if you want to come over," she said to Sara. "Just drop us a note and you'll have the ticket by return!"

"I won't forget," Sara promised. But even as she did so she knew it would be a long time before she set foot in America again. There was so much of the world she wanted to see, so many other things to do.

"I expect I'll be seeing you in London before you come back here," Mrs. Marriott said as she walked with Sara to the departure gate. "I'll be in London in the Fall and bringing Gina Banks with me. I've no doubt I'll be buying the Donnell Winter Collection too, so make sure Marc designs it with the American girl in mind."

"I could never tell Marc how to design anything," Sara said quickly. "He's a law unto himself."

Mrs. Marriott's look was humorous but the words she had been about to say were never uttered, for at that moment Sara's plane flight was called. There was another flurry of goodbyes and then she was walking across the tarmac to the plane.

The wind whipped against her skirts and tossed her red-gold hair high, causing her to run the last few steps. Once inside she took her place in her allotted seat and casually fastened her seat belt before settling back with a magazine her long legs crossed, her slim body at ease. How different she was today from the nervous girl who had made the flight three months ago. Unconsciously she had absorbed a great deal during her stay here and though she had always been eye-catching there was now an extra gloss to her appearance that made everyone look at her twice. Sara would have been stupid had she not been aware of this and yet, in some way, it did not make her conceited, only humbler, for she alone knew the effort that had gone into making little Sara Gay from Frimpton the brilliant product she was today.

The engine revved into life and the plane taxied across the runway. There was a gentle sensation of movement and they were airborne. Higher and higher they went, and within seconds she could glance out of the window and see New York thousands of feet below. Ahead lay the Atlantic Ocean and beyond it the familiar cliffs of England.

"Home." She breathed the word softly to herself. "Home and my family. Home and Marc."